THE WALLFLOWER'S SECRET

A REGENCY ROMANCE

ROSE PEARSON

LANDON HILL MEDIA

© Copyright 2024 by Rose Pearson - All rights reserved.

In no way is it legal to reproduce, duplicate, or transmit any part of this document by either electronic means or in printed format. Recording of this publication is strictly prohibited and any storage of this document is not allowed unless with written permission from the publisher. All rights reserved.

Respective author owns all copyrights not held by the publisher.

THE WALLFLOWER'S SECRET

PROLOGUE

The diamond pendant settled about her neck and a shiver ran down Julia's spine.

"Beautiful."

A little flustered, Julia settled one finger against the diamond and smiled at her mother in the reflection of the looking glass.

"I thank you, Mama. But are you quite certain that you wish to give me this? It is a family heirloom and I–"

"Deserve to wear it just as much as your sister did," her mother replied, firmly. "You are to be treated with the same kindness and consideration as your elder sister was given, my dear." The edges of her mouth dropped. "I am aware that your father can be a little gruff at times, and I am *certain* that you have overheard him muttering about your expenses and the like, but you are to pay no heed to that. You shall have a wonderful Season; you shall find a handsome gentleman and be just as contented and as happy as your sister."

"I do hope so." With a small smile, Julia dropped her

hand to her side and then let out a soft sigh. "I do look ready, do I not, Mama?"

"You look very well." Her mother turned and gestured to the door. "Come now. We must not be tardy."

The fluttering nervousness within her was like a dozen birds, all flapping their wings at once. Her cream gown swirled gently as she turned to the door and, with careful steps, Julia made her way to the staircase and then downstairs to the waiting carriage. Much to her surprise, her father, Viscount Harbison, stood there waiting for her. She had not expected to see him for, ever since their arrival in London some five days ago, he had been practically residing in his study.

"My dear daughter." Lord Harbison held out his hand and, with a glance to her mother, Julia took it. "How well you look."

Julia blinked in surprise at the compliment. In her entire life, her father had never once said a single word as regarded her appearance – neither good nor bad. In fact, he had always seemed disinterested in her appearance and, indeed, in her herself. Perhaps the prospect of having her gone from his house was enough to have his mood shift a little. That thought brought both a swirl of anticipation as to whom she might meet and, one day, perhaps even marry, as well as a tug of disappointment over her father's lack of consideration thus far. Regardless of her inner feelings, however, she inclined her head and managed to smile.

"Thank you, father. Might I ask if you intend to join us this afternoon?"

"No, indeed not!" Immediately, Viscount Harbison took his hand from hers and stepped back, as if he feared that she might grasp his arm and tug him forward. "I have far too much of my own affairs to consider at present, Julia. I am, of course, aware that your introduction to our Monarch is of the greatest importance, which is why I am so very glad that your mother will be there waiting for you. I look forward to your return and the Ball tomorrow evening. Thereafter, I will return to my estate knowing that your mother will be able to secure you an excellent match when the time comes."

Julia blinked away the burning heat behind her eyes.

"I quite understand, Father."

Her smile fell away as she turned, barely catching the murmur of encouragement her mother gave her as she passed. Stepping down the steps, she went to move forward to the carriage, only for something to strike hard at her. A cry erupted from her lips as she fell, the footman rushing forward to catch her. Hands helped her up and as Julia regained her composure, breathing hard and brushing down her skirts, the exclamations of both her mother and her father rang through the air.

"What can you be thinking of?" The anger in her father's tone took Julia a little by surprise, and she straightened quickly, seeing him storming towards a fellow who was, at that moment, attempting to pick himself up off the ground. "My daughter is, at present, on her way to her formal presentation to the Queen, and you have almost thrown her to the ground in your haste! Tell me, are you running from some sort of danger? Are you in fear for your life? These are the only two situations where I might forgive you for your heedless actions!"

"Your gown!" Her mother's gasp drew Julia's attention away from the gentleman, who was now brushing the dirt from his knees and apologizing profusely. "Look what he has done!"

Julia turned her head, her hand flying to her mouth as

she took in the small tear at the bottom of her gown. This was her presentation to the Queen, so she had to be nothing less than perfection.

"Whatever are we to do?" Wringing her hands, Lady Harbison looked helplessly back at Julia. "We have no time and –"

"Send for the maid." The fluttering nerves had turned into rolling waves, her breathing coming in ever quickening gasps. "She shall have to sew it as we make our way there. There is nothing else for it."

"That is a wise thought."

Putting one hand to her forehead, Lady Harbison closed her eyes momentarily, then, with a straightening of her shoulders, directed the footman to have Julia's maid join them, explaining what would be required of her. It was as these directions were being given that Julia permitted herself to look at the gentleman who had almost knocked her over. He was standing now, though her father was half a head taller. To her frustration, he had his back to her and she was not able, therefore, to see his face. She could not tell how he was feeling, or if there was any sense of embarrassment or regret within him, though, given the way that he stood with his head high and not dropping forward in the least, she presumed that there were no such feelings. Her father, on the other hand, was a picture of anger. Gesticulating furiously, he railed at the other gentleman, flinging one hand back in Julia's direction.

Julia watched carefully, wondering if the gentleman would turn around, approach her, and then offer his word of apology. He did not make any sort of movement in her direction, however, but instead inclined his head and made to step away - only to be held back by another few sharp words from Lord Harbison. Julia allowed herself a smile, both thankful and a little touched that her father had shown such indignation and anger on her behalf.

"Come, Julia." Having become a little distracted, it was only at her mother's urging and the touch of her hand on her shoulder that Julia made her way into the carriage. The maid, who had come rushing down the stairs at that moment, sewing basket in hand, quickly set to work, and Lady Harbison rapped on the roof of the carriage, ready to take their leave and leaving both Lord Harbison and the other gentleman behind, still in agitated conversation. "A most foolish gentleman." Lady Harbison clicked her tongue, looking out of the window as they rolled away. "I do wonder what he was doing, behaving in such a manner as that."

"I cannot imagine," Julia replied, trying not to move an inch as the maid's sewing needle began to glide through the fabric of her gown, though it was held carefully away from her legs. "I confess, I was a little surprised to see Father so angry."

Lady Harbison's expression softened.

"Your father loves you and wants your future to be a happy one." Lifting her shoulders, she let them fall. "He may not express it in so many words, but his actions have made that clear, I am sure."

"He certainly has." A gentle warmth began to rise up within her heart and, with a long breath, Julia settled back as best she could, her nervousness no longer as strong. "Might I ask if you know the name of that gentleman, Mama? Is he someone I shall see again? He certainly appeared to be dressed as a gentleman ought."

Much to her surprise, her mother looked away quickly, turning her head so that only her profile was visible to Julia. All the same, Julia could still take in the pull of her mouth and the way that her eyebrows dropped low.

"Yes, I know the name of that gentleman," she said, after a few moments. "His mother came out in the same year that I did. How sad she would have been, to see her son so reckless!" Julia frowned, questions beginning to pile up in her mind, though she spoke none of them. "The gentleman is known for his occasional bouts of foolishness," Lady Harbison continued, still looking out of the window rather than directing her attention to Julia. "I heard of it when your sister made *her* come out, and I was glad to warn her away from him – just as I shall do for you now. Many in society think him simply playful, a little troublesome, but meaning no harm - but I and your father would not consider him a suitable match for you. His title is suitable enough, certainly, and he is very wealthy also, but his character a little less than would be required."

"And what *is* his title?"

Lady Harbison cleared her throat gently and looked directly at Julia, severity burning in the grey orbs of her eyes.

"He is the Viscount Rushington," she stated, clearly. "And you are never to permit yourself to consider him, do you understand? Indeed, we will forget his very existence, now that I have warned you."

Julia blinked rapidly, her heart turning over upon itself, a little uncertain as to whether she felt a little afraid of the gentleman, or a trifle intrigued.

"Yes, Mama." The answer that was expected came quickly to her lips. "I promise you I shall never allow Lord Rushington to have any bearing upon my heart."

CHAPTER ONE

"Why do you appear so dusty?"
Benedict rolled his eyes.
"I had a strongly worded argument with the pavement."
His sister lifted an eyebrow.
"I assume that you lost the argument, then?"
"I did." Coughing to hide the swell of embarrassment climbing up his chest, Benedict looked down at his clothes. "It will be no matter. I shall change my attire at once."

He was not about to tell his sister that the reason he was so grimy was because he had been attempting to run to his townhouse and win the bet he had placed against Lord Burnley, who had stated that the carriage would be much faster - even at the busiest part of the day. Given the interruption, he had not only been shamefaced in losing the bet but also in appearing so dirty in front of his friends, and those who had come to watch the conclusion of the race. Thankfully all had dispersed, although, no doubt, there would be a few jibes thrown at him over the coming days.

"Good." His sister smiled briefly. "You do recall that we are to make our way to Lord Grifford's ball this evening, do you not? It will be an excellent one, I am sure." She eyed him carefully and Benedict looked away from her, eager to hide his expression. What he had shared thus far with one particular lady was not for his sister to hear of – not yet at least. The delightful Miss Davenport was, to Benedict's mind, the most beautiful, graceful, and amiable creature he had ever had the pleasure of meeting. Her sweet smile, whispering touches, and lingering glances over the last two weeks had caught his attention to the point of distraction. "You are not telling me something." Nell rose to her feet and shook her finger at him. "We have always shared every truth about our lives, have we not? Ever since we lost our dear Mama, we have found ourselves bound together, and I can tell that, at this moment, you are keeping something from me."

"Am I truly so obvious?"

Laughing, Nell set one hand on his arm, only for her smile to fade as she looked back into his eyes. At that moment, Benedict saw nothing but their mother standing there. Nell was like her in every way, from the searching blue eyes that spoke of the sky on a cloudless day, to the hair which would not sit as she wished it. Nell had the mannerisms of their mother in the way that she tipped her head to one side, putting her hands to her hips as she waited for some response – much as she was doing now.

"You are indeed, brother."

The question hidden in her words had his head dropping and he took a long, slow breath.

"I am to see a young lady this evening, that is all." Shrugging one shoulder when she quickly took in a breath, her eyes rounding, he struggled not to wave off her surprise. "Do not ask me her name, for the situation is not as easy as we might hope."

Nell frowned.

"What do you mean?"

"I mean I cannot tell you, little sister."

"Whyever not?"

"Because not every match is as simple as you and your Lord Oakes." Smiling, Benedict took her hand briefly. "But I will confess to being very much in love and I hope to introduce you to her very soon. Perhaps she will even be on my arm on your wedding day."

The widening of his sister's eyes spoke of her surprise on hearing him declare this, but she said nothing, much to his appreciation. She did not begin to throw questions at him, nor demand that he tell her the truth at once. Instead, with a nod, she merely turned away, but not before Benedict caught the glimmer in her eyes.

A sharp pain lodged itself in his stomach, and his smile fell away. Lord Oakes had been absent for some months now, having made his way across to the continent. His holdings there had required his attention, and he had wanted to deal with that before he wed Nell, so that he would not have to separate himself from her so soon after their marriage. It had been a wise decision, Benedict had thought, but all the same, he saw how sorrowful Nell was over her betrothed's absence. Coming to London for the Season had been his plan and, whilst Nell had been a little unwilling, he was glad to have insisted. The many joys she would find here would distract her from her sadness, albeit for a short while, at least.

"Are you going to stand here and stare at the wall, or are you to go and call your valet?"

The teasing words had Benedict starting, only to grin at his sister and then look ruefully down at his clothes.

"I think the valet," he replied, seeing Nell roll her eyes

and laugh. "Excuse me, my dear sister. I shall join you again shortly, for dinner and thereafter, Lord Grifford's Ball."

"Where I shall be watching you very carefully indeed," Nell warned him, her eyes narrowing a little. "I want to know who this particular young lady is."

"All in good time."

With a smile, Benedict excused himself and made his way to his rooms. The smile on his face lingered as he thought of Miss Davenport, a flurry of excitement growing in his heart. Very soon, he would see her again, would dance with her, and whisper all his longings to her waiting ears.

And see her dance with Lord Thomlinson also.

That struck the smile from his face. Grimacing, he rang the bell and then surveyed himself in the mirror. Miss Davenport had promised him repeatedly that she would soon be able to end her courtship with Lord Thomlinson. Her father had urged her towards the gentleman, but she felt nothing for him, not in the way her heart cried out with passion for Benedict. It would take a little time, she had said, and Benedict had promised that he would wait, swearing to her that his heart was hers to take. The sweet smile she had offered him in response seared through him whenever he thought of it.

It cannot be much longer. His chest rose and fell in a great sigh, urgency battling hard against patience. *Just a few more days and then I shall have all I have longed for.*

∼

"There you are."

Benedict put out one hand to Miss Davenport's arm, letting it slide gently down to her fingers so they might twine together with his for a moment. She looked up at him, her eyes holding the same flickering firelight as was in the lamps adorning the walls, her smile only adding to their brilliance.

"Here I am, Lord Rushington." The way her smile tipped to one side had his own eyebrows lifting. "How glad I am to see you this evening."

"It cannot compare to my own happiness." A little confused by the look on her face, he dropped her hand before anyone could see them. "What is it, Miss Davenport? You appear as though you have something to tell me."

The brightness of her smile grew, but she dropped her head so that her eyes were not holding fast to his.

"It seems that you know me very well indeed, Lord Rushington, and we have only been acquainted for a month."

Benedict chuckled, a faint hope beginning to grow.

"Then do share with me what it is you are thinking about, Miss Davenport."

"I shall." Her hand found his again. "It is with *great* sadness that I must inform you of a parting between myself and Lord Thomlinson."

Benedict's heart leapt up into his throat and, for a moment, he could not speak, his fingers pressing hers and expressing as much of his present emotions as he could.

"Is that so?"

"It is as I have said." Miss Davenport let out a long breath and shook her head, though Benedict caught the twinkle in her eyes. "It was very sorrowful indeed, although not entirely unexpected. My mother and father are both deeply disappointed, I am afraid to say." Her eyes slid to the left. "My mother is nearby, but currently in conversation with a friend, no doubt informing her of the pain I am in, at present, due to Lord Thomlinson's dismissal of my company."

"That is a struggle." Benedict pressed his lips together hard, sensing the swell of joy in his chest which might escape into a loud exclamation of relief, should he be even a little unguarded. "Might I ask what separated you?"

Miss Davenport's gaze rested down upon the floor.

"It seems as though he was somewhat unhappy with the company I kept at times and, when I stated that I would not give it up simply because he demanded it, he found that a little too much to bear. He decided that such a trait was entirely undesirable and thus, we stepped apart."

"Then I must ask you something." Benedict spoke quickly, and with a sudden urgency, fire building up within him, setting every part of him alight. "Miss Davenport, I do not ask you to court me, for I do not think that such a thing is required, not when we have been as we have these last few weeks."

A flush of color came to Miss Davenport's cheeks, her green eyes searching his.

"I do not fully understand, Lord Rushington. What is it that you desire then?"

"I desire to wed you."

The words came with such suddenness, Benedict could not have held them back, even if he had tried. A flicker of warning had his hand loosening from hers, his feet moving back as if he wanted to separate the two of them, only to see her smile.

That smile made him throw aside all caution. Squeezing her hand, he drew in air into starving lungs, only then realizing that he had been holding his breath.

"You wish to marry me?"

"I do."

It was not something he had considered before this moment, though betrothal had been in his thoughts, certainly. But never had he believed that he would propose to Miss Davenport the moment she was free from Lord Thomlinson – but now he had done so, it was too late to pull himself back from it. The way her eyes were shining with sparkling tears, the softness of her smile and the way she pressed his hand in return told him her answer before she even spoke the words.

"Of course I shall marry you, Rushington." A single tear dropped to her cheek and, with a small exclamation, she turned away from him, clearly desirous to hide her overwhelming emotions from the watchful eyes of the *ton*. "Forgive me, I confess to being a little overwhelmed."

"That is quite all right." If he were truthful, he would tell her that he too felt the very same way. A sweeping weakness ran from the top of his frame down to his feet and he put one finger to his collar, pulling it aside a little whilst being careful not to nudge his cravat. "I should go to your father. I –"

"No!" Without warning, Miss Davenport's hand shot out and grabbed his arm, her fingers tightening around his other hand as though she were attempting to keep him fixed in place. "Pray, do not."

"But I must." A little confused as to her response, Benedict frowned, looking down to where her hand encircled his wrist. "It is what must be done. I cannot marry you without his blessing."

"It is too soon." Miss Davenport's voice had grown quiet, and she released his wrist, her face a gentle shade of pink though her gaze remained steady. "Lord Thomlinson has only just separated himself from me. I cannot allow my father to think that I have behaved improperly by permitting the attentions of one gentleman whilst being courted by another!" Slowly, she pulled her other hand away from his. "Do you understand what I mean?"

Benedict tugged his mouth to one side.

"I understand that yet again, I am being asked to wait." Taking a step closer, he heard her catch her breath and smiled quietly, appreciating her response to his nearness. "First I have had to be patient as regards the situation with Lord Thomlinson and now, you ask me to wait again so that your father will be contented." Heaving a breath, he closed his eyes briefly. "It is just as well that I care for you as much as I do, Miss Davenport. You drive me to distraction but yes, I shall do as you ask."

Her eyes fluttered closed.

"I am grateful to you for that, Lord Rushington."

When they opened again, he gazed into the deep green of her eyes, the color reminding him of the lush green meadows he had run through as a child. The sweeping smile had his heart crying out for her but, pulling his hands into fists, he stepped back from her and inclined his head rather than pull her into his arms. Their interest in each other had been short lived thus far, but his strength of feeling was so overpowering, it commanded him.

"You shall dance with me, however?"

A quiet, tinkling laugh followed by the slipping of her dance card from her wrist was his answer. Heedless as to what society might think, he took both the cotillion and her waltz, handing it back to her so their fingers brushed lightly together. How he hoped she felt the same urgent swell of longing within her heart as he did in his!

"I look forward to our dances."

The words held more meaning than he could express, but by the way her smile grew, sending light into every part of her features, he knew that she understood what he meant. The need to hold her close, to have her in his arms and to be as alone with her as he could be, even if for only a few short minutes, grew all the stronger with every step he took away from Miss Davenport and it was all he could do not to turn around and thrust himself back into her company once more.

But now I am betrothed.

A thrill of delight ran up his spine and he grinned, his eyes sweeping around the ballroom as his heart lifted towards the skies.

I am betrothed and soon, I shall call Miss Davenport my wife.

CHAPTER TWO

*J*ulia dropped into a curtsey.
"I am very pleased to make your acquaintance, Lord Westfield." She turned to the young lady beside him. "And I am delighted to be introduced to you also, Miss Glover."

"As am I to you." Miss Glover glanced up at her father. "Father, might I take Miss Morningside to the gardens? They are so very beautiful this evening."

Lord Westfield looked to Julia's father, then, seeing him nod, assented.

"Yes, you may do so but do make sure to take your mother with you." He nodded in the direction of the door which led to the gardens. "I can see her standing by the door and she will, of course, wish to accompany you."

"Thank you."

Julia smiled at her mother, glanced at her father, and then stepped away with Miss Glover, who appeared to be more than a little delighted to have made a new acquaintance.

"I cannot tell you how glad I am to have met you." Miss

Glover quickly threaded her arm through Julia's, leaning her head a little closer to her. "My sisters have all had their Seasons and I have been waiting ever so long for my last sister to find her match! My father is quite stern about these things, you understand. He insisted I could not make my come out until all of my elder sisters were wed."

Julia smiled in understanding.

"I have had to wait until my elder sister wed also, though I only have the one – and now my own father, having made certain that I have made my come out, intends to return to his estate, stating that he has much more pressing matters to deal with there." She laughed and shook her head. "How many sisters do you have?"

"Six." Miss Glover heaved a sigh, her shoulders rising and then falling. "You can imagine my frustrations! Yet now, here I am, determined to make a good match before my father decides that I am to be a spinster and sends me to look after Francesca's children – she is my eldest sister, and already has three children of her own!"

Julia laughed, already enjoying Miss Glover's company.

"I am certain that such a thing will not occur," she stated, firmly. "No, indeed, you shall find yourself a husband this Season, I am quite sure of it."

"You *are* kind." Miss Glover tapped the arm of a lady as they passed, one with the same dark gold curls as Miss Glover, albeit with a little silver threaded through them, but continued on out into the gardens without so much as stopping to introduce Julia to her. "I am much too talkative, I am afraid, and my mother continually berates me for having *far* too much to say. She says I shall never find myself a husband if I do not stop talking, and that the very least I can do is to quieten myself until I am wed. Thereafter, she states, it does not matter how long I talk for. I shall be wed and settled, and nothing can be done about that." Her lips twisted in much the same way Julia's stomach did. "Though I do not like the idea. I think to hide my true character from the gentleman I am to call husband would be most unfair."

"I find that I agree."

Julia made to say more, only to come to a sudden stop as she looked all around her. Miss Glover was saying something more, no doubt something about the gardens, but Julia was much too caught up to take it in.

Lord Grifford's gardens were some of the most beautiful she had ever seen. The light of the April sky was dimming quickly, but the flickering lanterns lit up the spring blossoms beautifully, giving each a gold shimmer. A few trees spread out their branches, sending shadows dancing here and there as a soft wind joined in, whispering gently around Julia's bare arms.

"It is beautiful."

"I quite agree."

Much to Julia's surprise, a deeper voice than that of Miss Glover's answered her remark and, starting in surprise, Julia quickly realized that Miss Glover was no longer holding her arm as she had been, only a few moments ago.

"You need not be afraid, I am no scoundrel." The gentleman chuckled, his encouraging remark doing nothing to calm Julia's fright. "And your friend is only a few steps away, over there." Stretching out his hand, he pointed Miss Glover out and Julia forced herself to breathe a little more easily. Miss Glover was only five steps away, talking to another acquaintance, although Julia could not recall her stepping away from her. Her next thought was one of concern also, for could she be certain that Lady Westfield had come out with them? Yes, she had seen Miss Glover touch her mother's arm, but that did not mean the lady had followed them. She dared not even look at the gentleman for etiquette dictated that she be introduced before falling into conversation with him. "You are more well-mannered than I for I ought not to be speaking with someone I am not introduced to, is that not so?" As if he had been able to look into her mind and see the worries rising there, the gentleman had placed a finger directly upon her concern, his words pressing it back. "As I have said, I am no scoundrel. I am, however, glad to hear a young lady such as yourself express appreciation for these gardens. I think them quite beautiful also."

Julia, putting one hand lightly to her stomach to quieten the concern growing there, managed to respond, and was relieved when her voice was steady and calm.

"Yes, I do think them lovely. The reason I am standing here is simply because I was struck by the beauty. It was unexpected."

"Lord Grifford has always put a great deal of time into his gardens, both at home and in London."

"Then you are acquainted with him?"

Finally, Julia turned her eyes to the gentleman but found his features mostly covered in shadow. The flaming lamp near her sent a few flickers of red and gold across his face, but all she could see was the gentle swell of color in his eyes and the angular line of his jaw.

She pulled her gaze away again.

"Yes, Lord Grifford and I have been long acquainted, before he was wed to Lady Grifford, actually. We were at Eton together."

Julia considered quickly. The gentleman must be a few years older than herself, for as they had been driven to the Ball, her mother had stated that Lord Grifford was now one and thirty, and had only been wed some two years ago.

"I see. You have had a long acquaintance, then."

"Indeed." There was a note of humor in the gentleman's voice now, and another glance towards him caught the wide smile spreading across his face as though somehow, he knew what she had been thinking. "I myself am unwed, however. Lord Grifford has found that happiness before me, though I do not think it shall be too long before I too find myself at the altar." The heat in her face grew to such proportions that, had she been inside, Julia would have pressed both her hands to her cheeks in the hope of cooling them a little. She did not know what this fellow meant by saying such things but surely it could not have anything to do with *her*? In such a light, he could not see her features and since, to her knowledge, they were not acquainted, he surely could not be speaking of matrimony with her! So what was it he was speaking of? "I should take my leave."

Before Julia could say anything more, the gentleman had melted away into the gardens and she was left entirely alone. A little surprised at how quickly her pulse was threading through her veins, she hurried forward to stand again with Miss Glover.

"Ah, you have regained yourself at last." Miss Glover laughed and then gestured to the young lady and a gentleman standing beside her. "Might I introduce an acquaintance of mine? This is Miss Forrester, daughter to the late Viscount Rushington."

"I am very pleased to make your acquaintance." Julia dropped into a curtsey and tried to take the lady in, finding herself still a little on edge after her unexpected interaction with the shadowy gentleman. "Have you been in London long?"

"For *far* too long," Miss Forrester sighed, her features revealed by a sudden strength of light from the flames burning in the lamp only two feet away from them. "My brother dragged me here practically the moment that my betrothed took his leave of England."

A little surprised that such a vast amount had been revealed to her so quickly, Julia glanced at Miss Glover, only to see her new acquaintance nodding sagely as though she understood everything.

"And when do you expect his return?"

A weighted sigh left Miss Forrester's mouth.

"I cannot tell you. My last letter from him stated that I was to expect his return at any moment but, thus far, he has not arrived. My brother is very good at encouraging me and attempting to distract me by all manner of things, and thus far, I do find my sadness at our parting a little lessened."

"Then he is a good brother, I think," Miss Glover stated firmly, as Julia only nodded, realizing quickly that Miss Glover and Miss Forrester were well acquainted. "I am sure that you shall find yourself wed very soon."

"I shall be wed within the week of his arrival for the banns have already been called." Miss Forrester tried to smile, though Julia was sure that she saw a glimmer of tears in the lady's eyes. "It is very difficult to be patient."

Julia nodded fervently and looked away, thinking about how she had been forced to wait for her sister to wed, and how those three long years had been a very difficult torment indeed.

"I shall be glad when I hear your happy news," Miss Glover reached to take Miss Forrester's hand as Julia returned her attention to them. "Do excuse us, however. I should return Miss Morningside to her mother, for I did promise my dear father that I would not be long."

"But of course." Miss Forrester inclined her head and

smiled at Julia. "I am very glad to make your acquaintance. I do hope to see you again soon."

"As do I you."

Julia smiled warmly and then turned away, falling back into step with Miss Glover who took her arm once more.

"Miss Forrester is a lovely creature." A small sigh escaped her. "I do hope that her betrothed returns soon. It is very clear how much she loves the gentleman."

"It is," Julia glanced back over her shoulder. "Her brother sounds to be a very kind fellow also."

Miss Glover tipped her head and paused for a moment, the light of the ballroom now illuminating their faces.

"You are not yet acquainted with Lord Rushington?"

The name sparked a sudden memory and Julia's eyes flared, a twist of concern running through her.

"No, I am not. However, I have been told –"

"I am sure that you have been told many things," Miss Glover interrupted, with a smile. "And I am also sure that most of it is quite true. He can be a gentleman unguarded, often unwise in his actions, and inconsiderate of the feelings of others. However, I do not think that he means any great harm by it. He seeks to find laughter and joy in the mundane moments of life, but can be a little foolish with it." Her eyes glinted. "Should you like me to introduce you to him? I am acquainted with him, and you should then get to see – and consider him - yourself." Giggling, Miss Glover's eyes darted to the left and to the right before she leaned forward, her voice now a little lower. "He is, as you might expect, ridiculously handsome and, thus far, entirely unattached."

Without warning, a great and urgent desire to meet this interesting gentleman swept through Julia like a wave of heat. It pushed upwards, building words of acceptance as she opened her mouth to answer. Lord Rushington sounded to be a very intriguing gentleman, albeit a somewhat foolish and possibly imprudent one at times. Despite her mother's warning, there could be no harm in just being introduced to him, surely?

A movement behind Miss Glover caught her attention and, in an instant, all thought of meeting Lord Rushington drained away.

"My mother comes to find me, I think." With a set of her shoulders, Julia tried to push aside the sense of disappointment that ran down her frame in icy rivulets. "I should tell you now, Miss Glover, I have promised my mother not to have any involvement with Lord Rushington. Though perhaps you might point him out to me whenever we next meet?"

Miss Glover giggled again but hid the sound with her hand just as Lady Harbison came to join them.

"I was looking for your mother, Miss Glover. Is she with you?"

The flash of concern on Lady Harbison's face was quickly smoothed away when Miss Glover turned to indicate where her mother stood, not three steps away from them. Julia glanced around and was quickly borne away by her mother to be introduced to the lady. As she curtsied and greeted Lady Westfield, Julia allowed her thoughts to linger on the mysterious Lord Rushington, silently wondering to herself just how handsome the gentleman truly was.

CHAPTER THREE

Benedict made sure that he was standing tall, letting his gaze run over the gathering crowd. Having arrived a little earlier than usual at the Ball, he now stood by some tables and chairs, which were on a platform a little above the dance floor. Every one of his senses was heightened, his ears taking in every sound, the scent of lavender and rose mingling together as numerous ladies passed him by. The tips of his fingers were tingling in anticipation of capturing the hands of Miss Davenport, his heart thrumming furiously as he waited for her arrival.

"I am surprised to see you so captivated, brother."

Benedict started in surprise, then grimaced as his sister lifted an eyebrow.

"I did say that I would be watching you, did I not?"

"Yes, but I did not think that you meant it."

Nell laughed and came to stand beside him.

"Miss Davenport is to arrive soon, I think."

Benedict's breath hitched, swirling around in his chest as his head swung towards Nell, who was doing nothing other than looking out across the room, just as he had been doing only seconds ago.

"You need not ask me how I know," she told him, her eyes still on the crowd rather than looking at him. "Though I did notice how you lingered on the dance floor on two occasions at the ball we attended last Thursday evening. I confess that I thought the lady was already being courted by another. It is not as though I am acquainted with her, I should say, but only that the whispers were that Lord Thomlinson was taken up with the lady."

Seeing that there was nothing he could do but tell his sister the truth, Benedict folded his arms over his chest.

"Yes, my *dear* sister, you are quite correct. She *was* being courted by Lord Thomlinson, but that connection has been broken."

"By you?"

Nell swung towards him, but Benedict quickly dismissed her concern with a shake of his head.

"No, I believe that he found something displeasing about her character, though what it could be, I cannot understand." A small smile broke across his face at the thought of Miss Davenport, only for it to be pushed aside as his sister arched an eyebrow. "We are waiting a short while before we announce our betrothal."

Nell's gasp of astonishment brought a rush of heat to Benedict's face, and he closed his eyes, groaning.

"I forget. I had not told you of that."

"No, you had not." Nell's voice was suddenly very difficult to hear, one hand clutching at her chest in obvious shock. "My dear brother, far be it from me to tell you what you ought to do, but do you not think this a little hasty? You cannot know the lady very well as yet, surely?"

"I have known her a month." Skin prickling from the

doubt that flared in Nell's eyes, he shook his head at her. "Your concern has no foundation. My dear Miss Davenport has known from the very first moment of our meeting that we should be wed, just as I have done."

A trickle of uncertainty ran down his chest into his heart, but he ignored it as best he could. If he were to be entirely honest, he had not heard those exact words from Miss Davenport, but he was certain that she *felt* them. After all, she would not have accepted his proposal with such enthusiasm had she not been of the same mind!

"You have been acquainted with her for a month and, within that time, found yourself with very few occasions to be in her sole company." Nell put one hand to his arm, turning to face him now, rather than looking out across the room. "Rushington, I must offer you my concern regardless, even if you do not wish to hear it. I think you are much too eager in this."

Benedict let out an exasperated breath and Nell's hand fell away.

"My dear sister, you are to be wed soon. Surely you can understand the depth of feeling presently within my heart!"

"I can," she answered slowly, her eyes fixing to his, "but the love in my heart for Lord Oakes came from a long time spent in his company. We were acquainted and thereafter, we courted. We were able to spend time alone together – well, as alone as we were permitted – but had a good many conversations within that time. Might I ask how often you have spoken to Miss Davenport without any interruption from any other?"

Benedict opened his mouth and then closed it again, his conscience refusing to permit him to lie. Seeing his sister waiting, he scowled.

"We have had a few occasions for brief conversations."

"But nothing prolonged? Nothing where you might truly get to know her character?"

The scowl on his features grew in strength.

"I do not need to know her character. What I do know of her is more than wonderful. There can be no doubt over her character. It will be as beautiful as her face."

"I believe that you are mistaken there – though that is not to say that her character will *not* be as you believe it. It is a mistake to believe that you do not need to know her character fully. You cannot truly be in love with a lady if you do not know her as she is." Benedict was forced to fight hard against his sister's words, for they pressed back against his determination to believe himself in love with Miss Davenport despite the concerns that Nell had laid out. Yes, if he were to be truthful, some flickering worries lit up within him like a candle, but he quickly snuffed them out again. What he knew of Miss Davenport was more than enough to draw him towards her. "Is that not your Miss Davenport arriving now?"

Nell touched his arm and gestured to the right side of the room, leaving Benedict to follow her direction. Looking over, his heart beginning to quicken itself, he settled his gaze upon the lady in question and, as he did so, a long and contented breath brushed out from his lips.

"Yes, there she is."

"Your betrothed."

Nell did not sound overly pleased to be using such a term, but Benedict nodded firmly and said nothing further. Instead, he simply allowed himself to gaze upon Miss Davenport, taking in her laughing smile, the way her eyes danced across the room, her fan held in one hand as the other was given to a gentleman who came to greet her.

His smile grew fixed as the gentleman lingered a little

too long, his lips appearing to be pressed hard to Miss Davenport's hand. Miss Davenport was not frowning nor appearing to be in any way upset by the gentleman's attention but rather, when the fellow finally lifted his head, she was smiling at him, her cheeks a little red.

"Whoever is that fellow?"

Benedict moved forward but Nell put one hand to his arm, holding him back.

"Do not storm across the room, Rushington." Her warning was the only thing that held him back, his eyes narrowing as the gentleman continued to hold Miss Davenport's hand in his. "If your betrothal to Miss Davenport is not yet known, then you must expect other gentlemen to show her particular interest, must you not?"

Benedict closed his eyes to shut out the sight of Miss Davenport being so accosted.

"It must be very difficult for her also," he found himself saying, the words bringing him a little comfort. "To know that I am here, waiting for her, and yet to be so caught up by another must be –"

"And yet another."

Hearing the swell of darkness in Nell's voice, Benedict opened his eyes and first looked at his sister, seeing the frown that now drew her eyebrows together. He was about to ask what the matter was, only to look across the room and see Miss Davenport now in the company of not one, but *three* gentlemen. Her mother was nearby, but stood with her back to Miss Davenport and thus, was either entirely unaware of such behavior or was encouraging the attentions of such gentlemen to her daughter by her inattention. Benedict was not certain which.

"It is, as you have said, something I ought to expect."

Nell did not respond but from the slant of her mouth,

he could tell she was a little frustrated. It was, he supposed, a little disconcerting to see his betrothed so surrounded but, since their betrothal had not been declared openly, it was not something he could speak to.

Then, Miss Davenport took the arm of one of the gentlemen who quickly led her away from the rest – but not towards the dance floor. Before he had even thought of doing it, Benedict found himself striding out after her, cutting through the crowd of gentlemen and ladies and going in search of the lady he loved. The gentleman had led her away from her mother, which was, of course, entirely improper and Benedict's mind was already whirring with concern. Where was this gentleman taking her? No doubt Miss Davenport would be greatly perturbed and confused as to where she was being led, which meant he *had* to find her.

Pushing through one door and then another, he stopped so sharply, if was as if he had slammed hard into a wall. Gulping air, he stared, transfixed, at the sight of a gentleman with his arms around a young woman, who was looking up into his face with such a bright smile that the edges of it reached out to touch Benedict himself. The pain of it was so great, it was as if someone had struck him forcefully across the face.

Heaviness settled in his chest, weighing him down. He could not move, could not lift one foot from the floor, but could only sway a little, squeezing his eyes shut as if hiding the sight of Miss Davenport in another's arms would make it disappear completely.

It did not.

When he cracked one eye open only a few seconds later, she was still there and this time, her tinkling laugh scurried towards him, crawling over his skin and tightening his throat. Finally, he was able to move back, his steps soundless as he walked with great slowness back the way he had come. Pushing open the door, he stumbled a little as he stepped back into the noise and the light and the laughter that came from the others present at the Ball.

Nell rushed over to him, her eyes wide and her cheeks a little red.

"What happened?"

"It is of no consideration." The low, dull tone of his voice echoed out towards her, but his eyes fixed themselves on the floor rather than looking up at Nell's face. "I am to take my leave, Nell. I am sorry if you wished to linger a little longer but –"

"No, of course not, brother."

Her arm went through his and she began to step forward as though leading him to where he had to go. She did not ask him any questions but, as they made their way from the ball, Nell looked over her shoulder as though she might find the explanation of what had troubled him so.

Benedict said nothing, his heart aching and sinking lower with every step he took. This evening had been one he had thought would be full of nothing but enjoyment, laughter, and delight as he found himself in Miss Davenport's company once more. Instead, it had done nothing other than shatter his heart to pieces.

CHAPTER FOUR

*J*ulia inclined her head.
"I thank you, Lord Charleston. I should be delighted."

Slipping off her dance card, she handed it to the handsome gentleman, giving a glance to her mother who offered her a small, encouraging smile. Lord Charleston was very handsome indeed, with his light brown hair sweeping across his forehead and warm smile that sent sparks dancing across his hazel eyes. Their introduction had been made by Lady Westfield, who had then quickly stepped away, her task completed.

"The polka?"

"I do very much enjoy the polka." Accepting her dance card back from him, Julia inclined her head a little. "I look forward to our dance together, Lord Charleston."

"As do I. It will not be too long from now, so I shall very soon return to your company, Miss Morningside."

Smiling, she watched him take his leave, only for her gaze to catch upon another gentleman. He was standing to one side of the ballroom at Almack's, leaning heavily against one of the pillars that adorned the sides and the back of the room. His square jaw was tight, his gaze fixed, and his dark hair seemed to cast a shadow across his features.

For whatever reason, he was scowling at her.

Blinking, Julia swallowed and looked away, wondering at the gentleman's response to her. Whyever was he behaving in such a way? She was not acquainted with him, and certainly had done nothing to garner such a look of displeasure! Another glance told her that he was still there, still fixing his sharp gaze upon her, and still permitting his mouth to flatten into a thin line whilst his eyes narrowed a fraction. A chill ran across her skin, and she shivered lightly before turning around completely, cutting him from her view.

"Lord Charleston is a Viscount with good standing, good character, and an excellent fortune. When Lady Westfield mentioned him, I did ask if she might make the introductions, and I am very pleased that she has managed to do so."

"Does Miss Glover not consider him?"

Lady Harbison shook her head.

"Apparently not. Miss Glover stated that she found him too dull for her taste, from what I understand, though I cannot see why she would say such a thing. He is a gentleman, well-titled and wealthy. There can be nothing dull about that!"

Julia hid a smile, but nodded instead, wanting to make certain that her mother saw her agreement. Over the last ten days, she had spent a good deal of time with Miss Glover, to the point where she would now consider her a friend. Miss Glover was very fixed in her opinions when it came to the gentlemen of London *and* who would be a suitable match for her and her strength and determination. Julia had certainly been interested to hear her thoughts.

"I think that Miss Glover is set upon a love match, Mama."

Lady Harbison tutted lightly.

"That may be so, but a desire for such a thing is no promise of gaining it!" She looked sharply at Julia, her eyes searching her face. "Are you eager for that particular type of match also?"

"No, Mama."

The truth was Julia had given very little consideration as to whether or not she sought a love match. She had simply been delighted to be in London and to be permitted to now dance and converse with the various gentlemen who would be present for the Season. What she desired in terms of her own match was not something she had given much thought to, though Miss Glover believed it the most important of all things.

"That is a relief." Lady Harbison let out a long breath of obvious relief, her shoulders dropping a little. "It is a good deal more difficult to find a love match, my dear. If you are contented with a gentleman who will be kind, who will treat you with care and consideration, and who will have enough of a fortune to keep you in a good style, then that will do very well for you."

Julia nodded and made to agree, only for Lord Charleston to appear by her elbow, a small smile growing on his lips as she looked up at him.

"A very short time indeed, Miss Morningside," he laughed when she blinked in surprise. "The polka has just been announced. Are you ready?"

"Oh, of course." Seeing the warm smile of her mother,

Julia turned and accepted Lord Charleston's arm. "Forgive me, I had not expected it to be upon us so soon!"

Lord Charleston chuckled as he walked out with her to the center of the dance space.

"The polka is a very enjoyable dance, I think. And you will be relieved to know that I have not stood on any toes of late!"

Laughing, she made to say that she had no fear of such a thing, only for a strong hand to grasp her arm.

"I am surprised that you would *dare* to show your face here." Astonished, Julia reared back, blinking rapidly, as the gentleman she had seen glaring at her from across the ballroom now stood before her, swaying a little from one side to the other. Her hand clamped itself strongly around Lord Charleston's arm, her heart beating wildly as she stared at the gentleman, seeing his wide eyes and his hand pointing at her. "After what you have done, I would have thought that you would have hidden yourself away, far from where society could reach you. The audacity of your presence is –"

"Pardon me, but I do not know what you speak of." Heat built in her face as she waved him away, aware that his voice was loud enough now to carry to the very edges of the ballroom. Despite her fright, she drew herself up, realizing that there had been a misunderstanding as to who she was, but also seeing the need to defend herself. She did not want the *ton* to believe what was being said of her. "You mistake me for someone else. Do excuse me. I am to dance with Lord Charleston."

To her horror, the gentleman grabbed her hand and held her back, leaving her pulled between two gentlemen. The weight of his words flung themselves at her one at a time, stacking up one on top of the other, pushing her into the floor.

"You have cheated me, who dared to have an affection for you." His eyes narrowed, venom spitting from each word he spoke. "You stepped into the arms of another, even though we were betrothed."

"Come away."

A lady hurried to the gentleman, taking his arm, just as another protest broke from Julia's lips. Upon hearing it, the lady sent her narrowed gaze in Julia's direction, her face a little flushed, but her eyes sparking with fire.

"How can you protest? It is just as he has said!"

To Julia's dismay, it seemed as though this lady also had mistaken her for someone else, though she, at least, did not seem to be in her cups. Her words brought just as much shame and mortification as the gentleman had done and, with her face burning, she attempted yet again to defend herself, fearful as to just how many of the *ton* were now listening to this exchange.

"I have done no such thing." Despite her attempts to make her voice as loud as his so it might also ring around the room, it was quiet and unobtrusive. "I am not acquainted with either of you."

This was met by a cacophony of cries from the gentleman and the lady, who both railed at her with the same fury and disgust. Julia tried again to explain, to say that she was not who they believed her to be, but despite her protests, they would not listen.

"Excuse me."

Shock ran up her chest and lodged in her throat as Lord Charleston quickly dropped her arm and stepped away without explanation, clearly unwilling to dance with her now. Seeing that she was to be left alone on the dance floor, surrounded by other couples who had come to dance, Julia pulled herself back, exclaiming all the more that she was not who they believed her to be, but neither the gentleman nor the lady listened to her. Their words combined into a fury, raining fire and shame down upon her head, even though she had done nothing wrong.

"Julia!"

The sound of her name had her spinning around, only to see her mother beckoning her to draw close. With the exclamations of both gentleman and lady following her, she hurried towards her mother, grasping her hands tightly just as tears began to burn in her eyes.

"They have gone," her mother murmured, squeezing Julia's hands tightly. "I was about to step forward and state that they were mistaken only to see Lord Charleston leave the dance floor – and you also." Julia tried to speak, but tears lodged in her throat and, to her shame, began to drop to her cheeks. "Now, do not cry." A handkerchief was pressed into Julia's hand as her mother bent her head a little, looking straight into Julia's face. "The *ton* will have heard a great deal, but they must not see you weep. if you do, they may think you guilty of whatever was being placed upon your shoulders."

"You did not hear?" Julia dabbed at her eyes, her voice cracking and rippling with emotion as her heart tore with a sudden pain. "The gentleman accused me of ending our betrothal or some such thing, asking me how I dared have such arrogance as to show my face here this evening. I do not know what he meant."

Lady Harbison nodded but closed her eyes, her lips pinched. She did not speak for some moments and, as Julia watched the play of emotions run across her features, she felt her heart beginning to sink low. There was no promise of relief, no assurance that all would be well. Instead, her mother remained silent, clearly thinking through what had happened and considering whatever consequences might now befall her.

"Let us take a turn about the room." With a sudden strength to her voice, Lady Harbison took Julia's arm and almost dragged her forward, her steps strong and determined. "I cannot quite believe what has happened to you! That gentleman, whoever he was, mistook you for someone else! It is foolishness indeed to think that you were betrothed to him, particularly when you did not know his name!"

It took Julia a few seconds to realize what her mother was doing. It was only when she attempted to mumble something in response, only to hear her mother begin to say the very same things again that she understood. Lady Harbison was speaking as loudly as she dared in the hope that those who had heard what that gentleman had thrown at Julia would understand his mistake.

Julia dared not even allow herself to think what would happen if the *ton* turned against her. Daring a glance, she saw the sharp, snapping eyes of Lady Duncastle... and her spirits dropped even lower. Lady Duncastle was well known to be nothing more than gossip and if *she* had witnessed what had taken place, then Julia feared her reputation would be quite ruined.

"Keep your head up as we make our way to the carriage. I think it best we take our leave." The muttered direction from the side of Lady Harbison's mouth had Julia's eyes closing briefly, pain beginning to spread out across her chest. They were to take their leave from Almack's, then. This was to be the moment they would return home and, in their stead, leave nothing but whispers. No doubt gossip would spread across the room like a fire, tendrils of flame burning her although she would be nowhere near it. "Courage, my dear."

Another murmur from her mother had Julia nodding in response, before lifting her chin and walking forward with slow, steady steps. Looking straight ahead, she did not allow her gaze to spin to either the right or the left but kept it steady and direct.

Finally, out of doors, the cool evening air beginning to cool her hot cheeks, Julia closed her eyes and let two questions ring around her mind.

Who was the gentleman who had railed at her in such an uncouth fashion? And who precisely did he think she had been?

CHAPTER FIVE

"You cannot mope, not on a day like this."

Benedict lifted his head and forced a smile.

"I am not moping." Leaning forward, he kissed his sister's cheek. "You look radiant, my dear." The wind brushed back a curl of dark hair from Nell's forehead, though her eyes remained solemn. "I think our mother would have been very happy with your choice of husband. It is clear to all of us how much he cares for you."

Nell smiled at him, a touch of color in her cheeks which had lingered there since she had given her words of promise to her now husband.

"I do wish Mama had been present, Rushington, but I am so very glad that you were here to witness my marriage. Thank you for leaving London and coming back to the estate so that I might be married at home. It means a great deal to me, though I can understand that this day must be a little painful for you." Her eyes softened. "You had thought to bring Miss Davenport with you to my wedding."

"Indeed, I had hoped to do such a thing." With a deep breath, Benedict sighed but turned his head away, a little surprised that the pain he had felt only a fortnight ago was now nowhere near as sharp. "Yet I will not think of that, only of the happiness you now have." Smiling, he turned his face back towards his sister, seeing Lord Oakes making his way back from the waiting carriage towards them, no doubt in search of Nell. "You will write to me once you are returned from your wedding trip, and settled as mistress of Lord Oakes' estate?"

Nell nodded and then leaned into her husband as Lord Oakes put one arm around her in what was a very obvious display of affection – most unexpected and yet understandable, given the circumstances.

"I was just saying to Nell that she is to be mistress of *your* estate now, Oakes, while my own will turn to rack and ruin due to her absence."

"There is a simple solution for that, my dear friend." Lord Oakes grinned, his eyes alive with obvious happiness. "You shall simply have to find someone to marry!"

Benedict tried to laugh, but the sound tore itself to shreds before it could leave his lips and, instead, he rasped a sound that was neither a laugh nor a sigh. Catching Nell's frown, he smiled instead and then gestured to the waiting carriage.

"Come, let's see you away." The carriage was already prepared, with Lord Oakes taking Nell to France for their wedding trip. "I am very glad to see you both so contented."

"I thank you."

Lord Oakes shook Benedict's hand again and then led Nell to the carriage. With a brief word of goodbye, Benedict waited until his sister and Lord Oakes were safely in the carriage before waving them both farewell. The carriage rolled away, and Benedict watched it until it turned the corner and was no more.

The last fortnight had hurried past in a flurry of activity. There had been muslins and gowns, various shops to visit, and people to speak with. Lord Oakes' return to England had brought with it Nell's wedding day and, with the banns having already been called, there was no need to delay. Since Nell was to be married at the parish in which she had been brought up, both she and Benedict had returned to his estate which, thankfully, was only a day's travel from London.

Now, however, Benedict was left with a choice - should he return to London or remain at his estate?

With a twist of his lips, he took in the scene before him. Behind him stood his manor house, tall and stately and, within it, a myriad of servants who were all ready and prepared to care for him and the needs of the estate. In front of him, there was nothing but the beautiful gardens calling to him, flowers swaying gently in the light summer breeze, their scents mingling in the air and adding to the sweetness surrounding him.

But I would be here alone.

The grimace which pulled at his mouth was a reflection of the ache in his heart. The truth was, he did not want to linger here at the estate without company. Now that the excitement of the wedding was over, what was left for him? Yes, he might consider a house party, or invite some of his friends to join him, but they would not be likely to do so, given the present attractions of London society.

Miss Davenport is still within society, however.

Benedict ran one hand over his face and allowed himself a groan of frustration. The last time he had seen Miss Davenport, he had been in a state of disarray. Having imbibed a little too much, he had seen her smile up at a gentleman upon whose arm she rested, and his anger had become too great. Before he knew what he was doing, he had been spitting furious words at her, his vision blurred and his steps heavy as he allowed all of his anger and upset free. His sister had done her best to pull him away, only to then join in with his exclamations - although quite why she had done so, Benedict was not yet sure. Nell had said something about Miss Davenport denying the charge he had set against her, declaring that she was not acquainted with them and thus, even Nell's temper had been too strong for her to hold in check.

Would Miss Davenport's presence in London be enough to keep him at his estate?

No.

Lifting his chin as though she were present, watching him, Benedict exhaled loudly. No, he would not permit Miss Davenport to keep him away from the other joys that society had to offer. Besides which, he considered, he no longer felt as great a pain over the loss of her company. Yes, the shock of seeing her in the embrace of another gentleman had been utterly overwhelming, but it no longer held him in so tight an embrace. In fact, she did not even torment his thoughts as she had done before. No, there was no reason for him to remain at his estate and allow the rest of the Season to pass him by. He would return, he would enjoy himself in the ways he had done before – with merriment, jocularity, and with the keen desire to forget about Miss Davenport entirely, so that she would become nothing more than a shadow, kept at the very edges of his mind.

∾

"You have returned, then."

Benedict sniffed and picked up his whisky.

"I had no intention of stepping away for good. I went to see my sister married and then returned here."

"Is that so?" Lord Burnley did not appear in the least bit convinced, given the way that his eyebrows danced a little above his eyes, stretching high. "You have no concern as regards Miss Davenport, then?"

Benedict winced. Lord Burnley was one of the few who had known of Benedict's intentions for Miss Davenport although now, he considered, there were more than a few other gentlemen and ladies who understood the connection, given his outburst.

"I care nothing for Miss Davenport." Tension rattled through his words, pushing them out a little more quickly than usual. "Nothing at all."

"Which is just as well, given that she is now betrothed." Benedict froze in place, the new revelation sending ice through his veins. When his heart remembered it was meant to be beating, it slammed against his chest so hard, he had to gasp in air. "You look a little pale."

"It is only from the surprise, I assure you."

Clearing his throat, Benedict looked carefully at Lord Burnley, for both he and his friend were well known for their teasing and jesting. It would not surprise him if his friend had said such a thing to gauge, by Benedict's reaction, whether what he had said about Miss Davenport and his lack of emotion regarding her was quite true.

"I am not lying." Lord Burnley shrugged, yawned, and sat back in his chair, the picture of innocence. "She is betrothed. All of the *ton* are speaking of it."

Benedict blinked quickly, then looked down at the table, his hand curling around his glass of whisky.

"Might I ask to whom she is betrothed?"

Lord Burnley frowned, his mouth pulling tight for a few moments.

"I believe it is… yes, it is to Lord Hogarth."

Throwing up his eyebrows in surprise, Benedict shook his head.

"Good gracious. Lord Hogarth? That is not a gentleman I expected."

"Nor I," Lord Burnley chuckled, the sound turning a little dark. "Lord Hogarth is very wealthy and well-titled, but he is at least fifteen years older than she, and has never been married before."

Attempting to shrug off the remark, Benedict coughed lightly and then took a sip of his whisky.

"Mayhap he saw something in Miss Davenport which he did not see in any other lady before this moment."

"Perhaps." Lord Burnley narrowed his eyes. "Might I ask you a question?" He continued without even waiting for Benedict to either grant him permission or refuse him. "Whatever happened? I thought that *you* were courting Miss Davenport. Before you left for your estate, I received your note stating that all was at an end between you, and that you might return to London once the wedding was over. I do not understand why you separated from each other."

A line drew itself between Benedict's eyebrows.

"You were at Almack's that evening, were you not?"

"What evening?" Lord Burnley's frown grew deeper still, grooves forming across his forehead. "I have been to Almack's on more than a few occasions this Season so far."

Sighing loudly, and in what he hoped was obvious frustration, Benedict flicked one hand at his friend.

"Do not be obtuse. You know very well the evening I speak of. The one where I spoke sharply to Miss Davenport as she stepped out to dance with another gentleman? I was most foolish, I do not mind stating that aloud to you! I walked across the room until I came face to face with her and, despite seeing that a dance was about to begin, I said some rather ugly things to her."

Lord Burnley rubbed one hand over his forehead.

"I do recall hearing of that but..."

The rest of the sentence fell away, leaving Benedict to frown into the silence. He waited for his friend to continue, but it soon became clear that Lord Burnley had no intention of saying anything more, given the way that he sipped at his brandy and then looked around at the rest of White's.

"If you are going to tell me that she obviously cared nothing for me, nor responded with sorrow over my anger and upset, then you need not do so." Still a little uncertain as to why his friend had stopped speaking so abruptly, Benedict rolled his eyes when Lord Burnley looked back at him. "I realize now that I gave my heart much too easily and did not seek out her character, as I ought to have done." A grim smile pulled at his mouth. "It seems that my sister was right after all."

"I believe that your sister is wise about many things." Lord Burnley smiled briefly but then looked away again. "I am sorry that Miss Davenport did not care for you as you did for her. That must be a pain unlike any other."

Benedict wanted to throw the remark aside, a harsh laugh ready and waiting to be delivered, but instead, he took a moment and then spoke truthfully. It was not often that he and Lord Burnley shared such vulnerabilities, but he did so now, thinking it only right to be honest with his friend.

"When I first realized it, it was as if everything around me grew so very cold, it flooded every part of my being, to the point where I could not move an inch. Since then, the cold has melted away, little by little, until I feel more or less returned to myself." This time, he did allow the brittle laugh to escape him. "I believed myself in love, Burnley. I realize now that it was not truly so – or if it was, only the very hint of it. Seeing my sister marry Lord Oakes showed me what love truly is. It is the willingness to wait, to show great patience, and yet suffer immense pain because of it. Love is not an infatuation, but rather a devotion, a care that goes beyond all other things. I could not speak to any of that when it came to Miss Davenport. I believed that the beauty of her face would match her character, but I was mistaken and, thereafter, bore the consequences of it."

It took a few minutes for Lord Burnley to find even a few words to respond. Swirling the brandy in his glass, he looked down at it and then back up to Benedict's face again, as though there was something he wished to say but could not find the words for. Benedict waited, a crawling embarrassment beginning to make its way up his back, fearful now that he had said too much, or that his words would only merit Lord Burnley's laughter, only for his friend to sigh and shake his head.

"I think that I shall never permit myself to fall in love, given how much you have endured." With a scowl, Lord Burnley shrugged both shoulders. "But be glad, at least, that you shall not have Miss Davenport's company in London any longer. She leaves for her father's estate by the end of this sennight, which means that you have the rest of the Season to enjoy without her." This brought such a broad smile to Benedict's face that Lord Burnley chuckled. "You see? You can have a little happiness after all."

"Perhaps." Benedict threw back the rest of his whisky and set the glass down on the table, eyeing his friend. "My friend, I have only just finished speaking of my own heart and shared with you a great many truths. You did not mock nor ignore me, for which I am grateful. However, I do think that there is something you have not yet shared with me."

Lord Burnley's frown returned quickly, sliding back across his face.

"What do you mean?"

"There is something you wish to say, but you have not yet shared it," Benedict stated, firmly. "Before you attempt to deny it, I can see it clearly in your expression, so might I ask you to be as open with me as I have been with you? What was it about Miss Davenport you wanted to say?"

It took Lord Burnley the rest of his glass of brandy before he finally answered Benedict's question. Impatience danced like an irritating fly and Benedict had to bite his tongue on more than two occasions so that he would not interrupt the silence which had fallen over their conversation.

"Very well, very well." As if he could sense Benedict's impatience, Lord Burnley waved a hand as he spoke. "It probably means very little, but I did wonder whether you were entirely certain that it was Miss Davenport you spoke to that night."

A nudge of concern pushed itself against Benedict's conscience.

"Of course I am."

"Are you *quite* certain?" Lord Burnley pressed, his eyes narrowing as he leaned forward across the table. "You say you were in your cups and –"

"You seem to think that it was not Miss Davenport," Benedict interrupted, the concern growing into a heaviness that began to push itself into his heart. "Why would you say so?"

Again, Lord Burnley paused, and it was all Benedict

could do to remain where he was and not to throw himself across the table, grab Lord Burnley by the collar, and shake him until he spat out whatever he was to say next.

"Because I am sure that Miss Davenport was not present that evening," Lord Burnley said slowly, his eyes swiveling up towards Benedict again. "I was not at Almack's that night. I was at Lord and Lady Venables' soiree. I heard about the commotion at Almack's, for a gentleman came from the Ball to join the soiree instead, and told us all. As I looked around the room, I am quite certain that I recall seeing Miss Davenport's face. She went very white indeed."

In an instant, Benedict's stomach lurched so strongly, he feared that he might cast up his accounts right there and then. Lord Burnley was saying something more, flicking his fingers as if dismissing all he had just said, but Benedict did not hear him. The words were nothing more than a buzzing in his ears. Surely it could not be! Surely he could not have spoken all of that harshness and fury towards someone who did not deserve it?

Nell was there. She spoke to her also.

That truth brought him no comfort. Yes, Nell had come to take him away from the dance floor and had, thereafter, spoken in defense of him, but he recalled immediately that she had never been acquainted with Miss Davenport, and had never been introduced. No doubt his sister had simply acted upon the assurance that the lady Benedict had been speaking to had been Miss Davenport.

What if he had been wrong?

Closing his eyes, he put his elbows on the table and dropped his head, gripping his hair with either hand. Squeezing his eyes tightly shut, he fought against the roiling of his stomach, but he could not prevent his heart from beating so furiously that it felt as if it might come right out of his chest.

If it was not Miss Davenport whom he had showered all of his frustrations upon, then who had it been? And what precisely had become of her?

CHAPTER SIX

*J*ulia dropped her shoulder and, thereafter, lowered her head.

"It does not matter, Mama."

"Of course it matters, my dear." Lady Harbison pulled gently back on Julia's shoulders so that her head lifted and her back straightened. "You must look your very best."

"Why must I? It is not as though anyone looks at me."

There was no answer from her mother for this statement, leaving Julia with a fresh heaviness upon her heart. These last two weeks, she had found herself shrinking back when in society, becoming nothing more than a whispered word among the *ton*. After the gentleman had scolded her violently in the middle of Almack's, she had been left reeling, forced to accept the consequences of something she had not done. What made the situation all the worse was the realization that the gentleman was not about to come back into society and state that he had made a mistake, thus releasing her from the guilt and shame which was not rightly hers to bear.

Had she seen him, then Julia had determined to speak

with him at once, to demand that he do what he could to help her, but there had been not even a single moment where she had seen him in amongst society. Her mother had spoken almost continuously about how she had not seen the gentleman clearly, and how much she wished she had, but to Julia's mind, such wishes were nothing but foolish. Nothing could be done. She was now to face a much darker future than she had ever anticipated, pushed back against the wall of London society and becoming nothing more than a wallflower, draping the walls and the streets of London without any real consideration from anyone.

"There are still many who look at you." There was no confidence in Lady Harbison's voice and when Julia looked at her mother, no smile came to either face. They both knew that the situation was very difficult indeed. "Oh, that I had seen the gentleman clearly and recognized his face." Her mother grasped both of Julia's hands, holding them tightly whilst a gentle gleam of tears came into her eyes. "I am so very frustrated that I did not look more closely."

A swell of love broke through Julia's pain.

"You did not do any of this, Mama. It is not your fault, and nor is it mine!" At such a statement, her heart ached all over again, and she lowered her gaze to the floor. "But you are quite correct. I must continue to go out into society in the hope that some gentleman might either ignore the rumors, or care very little for them."

Her mother drew in a long breath and put a smile on her face that brought no light to her eyes.

"Yes, that is it precisely. Which is why, as I have said, you must look your best."

Julia nodded and did the same as her mother had done, pressing a falseness to the curve of her lips and looking back at her reflection with nothing but doubt and sadness in her eyes. She would do as her mother had asked, would go to the soiree, and stand quietly to one side, seeing the other gentlemen and ladies go about as they would normally do, whilst she herself would stand further and further back, not invited into conversation with anyone. Should she attempt to join a conversation, as she had done before, the band of gentlemen and ladies would separate quickly and leave her with a clear impression as to their consideration of her. The whispers of her secret betrothal and her subsequent poor behavior with other gentlemen were thoroughly spoken of throughout the *ton,* though who it was she had meant to be betrothed to had varied wildly. She had heard almost every name possible, Julia imagined, for gossip wound lies within the words whispered from one ear to another.

It was all so very unfair – but there was nothing she could do about it.

"Do remember to smile."

Julia nodded and dutifully did as she was asked, taking out her fan and waving it gently in front of her simply so that she had something to do with her hands. To her surprise, someone paused to look at her, an older lady that Julia immediately recognized.

"Good evening, Lady Guthrie. I do hope –"

The lady turned her head sharply, her eyes pulling away and she immediately took leave of both Julia and her mother. It was very near the cut direct. Julia turned, looking to her mother and seeing the look of shock etching itself across Lady Harbison's face.

"Lady Guthrie has long been one of my acquaintances, I did not think that she..." Giving herself a small shake, she closed her eyes tightly but not before Julia caught the flash of pain in Lady Harbison's eyes. Julia wanted to say something, to do something which would aid her mother, but instead, she simply reached out and took her mother's hand, doing her utmost to ignore the slice of pain which had cut through her at Lady Guthrie's sharpness. "It is to be expected, I suppose."

"Yes, Mama." The thinness of Lady Harbison's voice revealed the depths of her sorrow and Julia fought to hold back fresh tears. "I am sorry."

Her mother sniffed and managed a watery smile.

"It is not your fault, my dear. I only wish there was something we could do."

"As do I."

Allowing her gaze to drift across the room, she did not allow her eyes to linger on any one face. It did not seem to make a single ounce of difference if she protested her innocence to anyone who would listen. She had already tried informing certain ladies that she was not at all acquainted with the gentleman who had spoken to her in such a stern and overpowering manner, but none would listen and had behaved much as Lady Guthrie had done. Her mother had attempted the same and, thankfully, had received a little sympathy from one or two of her friends – but their numbers were not enough to pull Julia back into the fullness of society. Now, she was left to stand on the side, no doubt to fade away until they either decided that she had completed her punishment or, more likely, until she was entirely forgotten.

Was that really a circumstance she was willing to accept?

Her gaze lowered to the floor.

What else am I to do?

"Miss Morningside, there you are."

Hearing her name spoken with such enthusiasm was so extraordinary that Julia's skin prickled, her heart lifting with a sudden hope.

"Miss Glover, how good to see you."

"I shall be nearby."

Her mother's voice murmured in Julia's ear as Miss Glover beamed back at her.

"I am delighted to see you again also. I have been absent for two weeks and have missed society greatly." Her smile began to fade away as she regarded Julia carefully. "You must be a little sorrowful at present, however. I was not at Almack's during that particular evening, rather, at a soiree instead, but of course, I have heard of what took place."

"And are you quite certain that you wish to be talking to me?" Julia let her shoulders drop a little. "Almost everyone within society thinks ill of me. I have protested my innocence to all who will listen, but they still insist that I am to stay in the background and no longer step forward as I once did."

Miss Glover touched her arm, her eyes rounding.

"Then you were not betrothed?"

Julia blinked, then threw up her hands.

"No, of course I was not betrothed! Everything that gentleman said to me was nonsense. He mistook me for someone else."

"I see. I was very confused over that, I must say. Now, you need not worry about my keeping company with you. I will explain all to my good parents, and they will be contented with that. Of course, I shall do my very best to put it about that you were not the person for whom Lord Rushington's words were intended."

At this, Julia's hand shot out and she grasped Miss

Glover's arm tightly, her pulse racing, her eyes wide and locked upon her friend. It took her a few attempts to speak clearly, such was the force of astonishment and relief which swam through her veins.

"You – you know the gentleman?"

"Of course I do. It was Lord Rushington who spoke to you and, thereafter, his sister - to whom you have already been introduced. I have been with them both recently, and the situation was mentioned briefly but it was clear that Lord Rushington did not want to speak much of it. To my shame, I did not say a word in your defense for I did not know the truth of the situation. How I wish I had done so, now!"

Julia blinked rapidly, recalling the name, and remembering the gentleman who had almost knocked her to the ground when she had been on her way to make her presentation to the Queen. That gentleman and the one who had railed at her furiously in front of all of society were, it seemed, one and the same.

Her eyes closed and she let out a shuddering breath, doing her best to keep back the tears which were building behind her eyes.

"I do not blame you in the least."

Miss Glover smiled warmly.

"I thank you. You are most kind." She took a breath and her smile dropped away. "Yes, it is Lord Rushington who spoke to you. I was surprised to hear that you were betrothed to him but, then again, after seeing you speak with him in Lord Grifford's gardens, I thought that there might have been a connection which I was unaware of, even though you claimed not to have his acquaintance."

"Speaking with him in Lord Grifford's gardens?" Confused, Julia put one hand to her forehead, trying to recall the moment Miss Glover spoke of. "I do not recall –"

"It was before I introduced you to his sister, Miss Forrester," Miss Glover explained, quickly. "You understand, now, my own confusion? I thought you to be already acquainted with Lord Rushington, perhaps secretly, and then I myself introduced you to his sister. When they spoke of what had taken place at Almack's, it never occurred to me to think that there might be a mistake for, to my mind, you were all aware of one another."

Julia closed her eyes and managed to push away the threatening tears.

"I understand." Recalling the night in question, she remembered the gentleman speaking with her, remarking on her quiet comment on the beauty of the gardens. She had never discovered the name of the gentleman, not until this moment. Little wonder that her friend had been confused as to what had taken place! "It was a dark evening. I did not recognize Miss Forrester when she spoke to me alongside her brother, even though we had been previously acquainted."

Miss Glover's eyes rounded in sudden understanding.

"But of course! Goodness, my dear friend, you have found yourself in a difficult situation, have you not? What are we to do about it?"

"What *can* be done?" Julia spread out her hands and sighed. "It has been two weeks since that incident and, in that time, Lord Rushington and his sister have made no effort to correct their mistake."

"Because I do not think that they were aware of it," Miss Glover interjected. "They have also been absent from London, for Lord Oakes returned – if you recall, he was Miss Forrester's betrothed – and the wedding took place shortly thereafter. It was at Lord Rushington's estate and, given that my parents and I were invited to the wedding, we were absent from London for a short while. Miss Forrester is now Lady Oakes, and I do not think she has any intention of returning to London within the year."

Julia's heart sank so low, it took every flicker of hope with it.

"And Lord Rushington himself was at his estate also, where perhaps he remains."

"He was still there when we took our leave. I do not know whether he intends to return to London." The sympathy etched on Miss Glover's face did little to encourage Julia's spirits, and she looked away, tears beginning to force their way forward again. "But if he is, I am *certain* that he will realize his mistake and make amends."

Julia shook her head and opened her eyes, unable to prevent a single tear from dropping to her cheek.

"I do not think that he will. Besides which, even if he was to attempt to do so, it has been two weeks since he made such a mistake. Do you think that the *ton* will listen to him?"

"Yes, I think they will." Miss Glover smiled in what was clearly meant to be an encouraging fashion. "We must pray that Lord Rushington returns to London, for you will then be able to approach him, state what you desire him to do and thereafter, see yourself restored to society. I think – wait!" Julia caught her breath, although she did not know what it was that had caught Miss Glover's attention. "Can it be?" Coming to stand directly beside her, Miss Glover gestured across the room, using only her chin, and a fixed gaze. "It is as though our discussion has brought the gentleman to us!"

A rush of nervousness immediately poured itself into

Julia's frame and she shivered violently, her stomach rising up while, at the same time, her heart dropped low. Looking across the room, she listened to Miss Glover's description of the fellow and finally managed to settle her gaze upon the right man.

Lord Rushington had a broad smile, blue eyes which were presently alive with laughter, and thick, dark hair which carelessly shifted this way and that across his forehead whenever he moved. He was of a somewhat stocky build, though not overly tall. This was the first time that she had been given an opportunity to study his features, for when he had almost knocked her over, she had only seen his profile and, during the incident at the Ball, his features had been so swept with anger, and she had been so overcome with fright and fear, it had been difficult to take him in.

Now, however, she had the opportunity to do so. Yes, he was handsome and certainly appeared confident, but those two accolades meant nothing to her. She wanted him to be a humble sort, to have concern about what he had done, and to be desirous to apologize to her, so that she might be able to return fully to society, instead of fading into the wallflower she was now expected to be.

"I shall speak to him." After speaking so decisively, Miss Glover stepped forward, but Julia put a hand to her arm and held her back.

"Wait a moment," she murmured as Miss Glover looked back at her with slightly widened eyes. "I have an idea I should like to discuss with you."

"Something as regards Lord Rushington?"

Julia nodded, a grim smile tightening her features.

"Yes, solely to do with Lord Rushington."

Keeping her gaze fixed to the gentleman, she began to explain precisely what she wanted to do and, as Miss

Glover nodded, a swell of determination began to grow. It pushed her forward, urged her on and gave her such a thrill of hope that, for the first time in as many weeks, Julia allowed herself to smile.

Perhaps all would not be lost after all.

CHAPTER SEVEN

"I must say, it is good to be back in London."
Lord Burnley chuckled.
"I think you only say such a thing because Miss Davenport is no longer present."

Benedict could not help his smile. The day was fine, and a walk through Hyde Park brought with it a good many delights. The sun was warm, the flowers glorious, and the stroll had, thus far, given him the opportunity to greet a good many acquaintances, all of whom had met him with a smile.

"Mayhap," he agreed, offering his friend a small shrug. "It may surprise you to know that, since I have returned to society, I have barely even thought of her. It does appear as though my feelings for the lady have burned up and blown away, without causing me a great deal of pain." Lord Burnley's eyebrows rose, although he said nothing, but neither did Benedict allow himself to take heed of his friend's response. "We shall have to think of something to do," Benedict continued, while his friend remained quiet. "Shall we place another bet, mayhap?"

At this, Lord Burnley grinned.

"Do you truly wish to embarrass yourself, yet again?"

Laughing, Benedict threw up his hands in mock frustration.

"If you recall, I was held up during our last bet, which is the only reason I lost. If I had not stumbled over that young lady, then I am *certain* that I would have beaten your carriage."

"Is that so?" Lord Burnley's grin grew a little lop-sided as he looked over at Benedict. "Then perhaps we should make the bet again, although this time with the wager amount doubled."

"Mayhap we should." Not in the least bit perturbed, Benedict let his hand curl tight in anticipation. It was time for a little joviality, for he had been much too serious these last few weeks. Now that the matter with Miss Davenport was at an end, he had time to find himself some new venture, and even to permit himself a little foolishness. Bets and wagers were nothing but moments of enjoyment and laughter, and he had no intention of holding himself back from such things any longer. "Mayhap we ought to consider a new wager." When his friend let out a bark of laughter, Benedict shrugged. "It is dull to repeat one, do you not think? I am certain that, by the end of our walk through the park, we will have come up with something entirely new."

"So this is your intention, is it? Just amusement?" Lord Burnley's grin had dimmed a little. "You have no thought of going in search of another young lady to betrothe yourself to?"

Benedict scowled and looked away from his friend, aware of the immediate rejection of such an idea within himself.

"No, I have no intention of doing any such thing. I shall

enjoy the remaining months of the Season and thereafter, return to my estate and resume the many laborious tasks which await me."

"As we shall all do." The darkness in Lord Burnley's tone spoke of the same discontent that Benedict felt when he considered returning to his estate and leaving good company behind. "So therefore, you are right to state that we must seek out as much enjoyment as we can." Turning his head, he coughed quietly, his eyes fixed on Benedict's. "Although might I ask if you have any intentions, with respect to the young lady you railed at, during the ball?"

In an instant, the scowl which had been on Benedict's features only deepened. Yes, he had been thinking of it, but, given the fact that he did not know who the young lady really was, as well as being aware that society would have moved onto something new by now, he felt himself a little lost.

"I am sure that society is speaking of another matter by now."

"Yes, that is true," Lord Burnley agreed. "They talk of Lord Kingshill and his ridiculous pursuit of Lady Woodridge, the widow to the late Earl of Woodridge."

Benedict nodded slowly.

"That is good." He turned his gaze fully to his friend. "Do you know the name of the young lady I railed at that evening?"

Lord Burnley shook his head to indicate no.

"It was not something which I considered of any great seriousness, so I have not asked a single question about it. And, as I have said, since the gossip has now moved on to something new – and something which I find interesting and am eager to listen to – the matter is quite forgotten, to my mind, at least."

A slight nudge of relief ran down Benedict's spine.

"So whilst I may have embarrassed the lady in question, the one I mistook for Miss Davenport, you do not think that the *ton* continues to laugh at her and my ridiculous behavior towards her?"

Lord Burnley shrugged.

"I cannot say, but I suspect that yes, what you say is correct. I am sure that all is well with her, and she is now more than relieved that the *ton* no longer think to discuss her. In fact," Lord Burnley continued, slapping Benedict on the shoulder. "I am quite certain that, if you were to ask a good many questions about who she was, to discover her and, thereafter, attempt to apologize, she might be mortified all over again, simply because you have brought the matter to the fore once more."

This conclusion calmed Benedict's guilt somewhat, and he released a long breath, his shoulders dropping.

"Then I too shall consider it at an end," he stated, firmly. "You are quite correct. It would be a mortification – both to her and to me."

"Very good," Lord Burnley grinned. "I think that I –"

His sentence was brought to an end as he – and Benedict also – were accosted by three ladies.

The first stopped by Lord Burnley and began to engage him in conversation, with two others separating themselves from the first and coming towards Benedict instead. The first he recognized as Miss Glover, someone both he and his sister were well acquainted with, given that their parents were known to each other also. The second, however, he did not know.

"Good afternoon, Lord Rushington!" Miss Glover spoke with her usual warmth and her usual speed, words quickly coming from her, one after the other. "I do hope that you are well? Your sister's wedding was quite delightful, and I can assure you of my pleasure in being there to witness her marriage! Are they on their wedding trip now? I do recall Miss Forrester stating that they were to go to France, although I might well be mistaken in that regard."

"No, you are not mistaken."

With a chuckle, Benedict reassured Miss Glover quickly but allowed his gaze to rest upon the other young lady. She was most direct in her gaze, looking at him with clear green eyes, her burnished curls dancing across her forehead as the wind chased them about. There was something familiar about her, but Benedict could not recall ever having been introduced.

"Pray do forgive me!" Miss Glover's hand flew to her mouth. "I am so terribly sorry, for I realize that I ought to have made the introductions by now. My friend has been eager to make your acquaintance, Lord Rushington, so I brought her to meet you."

A little flustered, Benedict looked down, then let his gaze lift back up to the lady, finding his senses stirred just a little.

"And why, might I ask, should you wish to be introduced to a gentleman such as myself?"

The lady smiled, but it did not send any sort of light sparkling into her eyes.

"Because I believe that we have already spoken, Lord Rushington."

"Oh?" Quickly, Benedict ran various situations and circumstances through his mind, trying to think of who this might be, and why she was so certain that they had spoken already. "I am afraid that I do not recall it."

"It was some time ago," came the quiet voice. "Lord Grifford's Ball? I was out in the gardens and spoke with you briefly – or should I say, you interrupted my quiet thoughts to tell me how much you thought of the gardens!"

At this explanation, Benedict realized at once what the lady meant, nodding urgently.

"Yes, I do recall." He managed a smile, silently acknowledging that he had interrupted the young lady that evening. Having stepped into the gardens, he had found himself a little entranced by her quiet murmuring and, seeing her standing alone, had taken it upon himself to join her. "Forgive me for my improper manner that evening. I ought to have found someone to introduce us but, given the situation, I dared to speak to you without introduction. I am glad that we have now had an opportunity to be properly introduced."

When she smiled, Benedict's heart leaped with such a ferocity that his smile became fixed. Why ever was his heart behaving so? He did not even know this young lady, save for the few words they had shared that night, so many weeks ago! Would he truly permit her sweet smile to affect him so strongly?

"I am glad that we have been introduced also, Lord Rushington. I do hope that you did not think me overly reserved. Young ladies, such as myself, must take the greatest care, you understand."

"I do." Much to Benedict's relief, his heart had decided to put itself back into place and was now beating just as it ought. "It was I who was at fault, though I must say, I was intrigued to see you so affected by the gardens. They were quite lovely, of course, but not overly magnificent. The Vauxhall Gardens are, by comparison, much more delightful and worthy of all manner of accolades."

The young lady lifted an eyebrow but did not smile, and the grin Benedict had been attempting to set upon his face slid away. He did not want her to think that he had been mocking her opinions or considerations, but perhaps his words had been a little harsh.

"I think that each person sees beauty differently, Lord Rushington." The green of her eyes darkened a fraction, only for her to then smile and chase the darkness away again. "But then again, I have not been to Vauxhall Gardens, so I suppose I cannot speak with any true understanding."

"Then you *must* attend," he said, long before he had even thought about stating those words. "There is to be a fireworks display in only three days' time and, at present, I believe that Madame Saqui is also amongst the attractions there." Seeing the young lady and Miss Glover share a glance, he quickly explained. "Madame Saqui is a tightrope walker, and her skills are quite a sight to behold! I was fortunate enough to see the entertainment only last Season. I should encourage you to attend if you can, Miss… Lady…?" Realizing that he did not know her name, he waited for her to give it, only for her to, yet again, look to Miss Glover.

"Shall *you* be present in three evenings hence, Lord Rushington?" The young lady tilted her head a little as she spoke, though he did not miss the touch of color in her cheeks. "Neither Miss Glover nor myself have attended such a performance in Vauxhall Gardens. It would be delightful to be there with someone who knew the Gardens well."

Benedict nodded quickly, only to then realize what he was doing. The young lady's expression lit up with a bright smile, and Benedict's heart twisted in his chest. He could not pull himself back from this now, not when she appeared to be so delighted.

How strange it was that his spirits were now lifting a little, also.

"I should be delighted to accompany both yourself and Miss Glover," he answered, as the two ladies smiled at him.

"I will be attending with my mother also, of course." Miss Glover gestured to the other young lady. "You may join us in our carriage if you wish?"

"Thank you. I would be glad to." Turning her smile in Benedict's direction, the young lady inclined her head though her eyes held fast to his, her dark eyelashes fluttering lightly. "You are very kind, Lord Rushington, to invite us. I am already looking forward to our time together."

"But of course." Clearing his throat, he clasped his hands behind his back, embarrassed to ask her for her name after such a long conversation, but seeing that he had no other choice since, as yet, Miss Glover had not said a word. "You must forgive me, but I realize that I do not recall your name."

"Is that so?" The young lady's eyebrows lifted high though, thankfully, she smiled with it. "That is not a particularly gentlemanly thing to do, Lord Rushington. I thought a gentleman was meant to play close attention to any new acquaintances so that a situation such as this would not occur!"

Benedict blinked, a gentle warmth beginning to pool in the pit of his stomach. Was she teasing him or laughing at him? From the way her eyes twinkled, he considered it was the former and allowed a small breath to escape before he answered.

"You are quite correct. It is, yet again, another fault I must apologize for."

"Your second, Lord Rushington." She emphasized his name, making it quite clear that she recalled precisely who he was. "However, I shall not be lenient with you, I am afraid. Instead, I shall leave you to suffer."

"Oh?" A little surprised by her response, but also at the way that her eyes danced as she spoke to him, Benedict put one hand to his heart. "And what is to be my punishment?"

A quiet laugh broke from her lips before she spoke, the sound sending a broad smile stretching wide across his face.

"You shall have to suffer for the next few days, searching your mind and your memory for the name which was given you. When we meet at the Vauxhall Gardens, you shall either greet me by my name or you shall not – and what happens thereafter shall depend entirely on your response!" With another smile, she inclined her head and then turned away, fluttering her fingers at him as she went. "Good afternoon, Lord Rushington."

Try as he might, Benedict could not help but let his gaze follow the lady as she walked away from him. To his surprise, she did not stop and speak with any others, though many ladies and gentlemen were walking through the park also, with some walking directly past her. A small smile plucked at his lips as he finally turned his head away from her. Exactly who was this mysterious young lady? And why did he now find himself so utterly intrigued by her?

CHAPTER EIGHT

The sting of forcing a smile she did not feel upon her face took some moments to fade.

"I do not understand fully what it is that you are trying to do." Slipping one arm through Julia's, Miss Glover glanced up at her, but then dropped her gaze to the path again. "I thought that we wanted only to see whether or not he recognized you."

"And it is clear that he does not." Julia spoke calmly but, inwardly, her emotions raged against one another, with each one competing for dominance. "I could see that from the moment that he first glanced at me."

Miss Glover's lips flattened as her eyebrows dropped low over her eyes.

"Yes, I would agree with you there. I confess that I was disappointed. I was about to tell him who you were but your hand on my arm stayed me. I do hope that I understood you correctly there."

Julia nodded.

"Yes, you did." Inhaling a breath of spring air, she closed her eyes briefly and then came to a stop, seeing a bench to her right and gesturing to it. "Do you mind if we sit for a moment? I feel a little fatigued after what has just taken place."

"But of course." Miss Glover's eyes flared with obvious concern, and she sat quickly, her hand not releasing Julia's arm until they were both seated. The maid Miss Glover had brought with them moved to stand unobtrusively next to a tree, perhaps seeking out a little shade on what was quickly becoming a rather humid afternoon. "I am sorry that he did not recognize you. If he had, then this might be a happier moment!"

"I appreciate your sympathy, Mary." Julia took a long breath, her hands curling together in her lap. "I could have given him my name, and looked then to see if there was any flare of recognition in his eyes but, as I was about to do so, I found that my desire changed."

"You wished to flirt with him?" The boldness of Miss Glover's statement had heat searing Julia's cheeks. "You did very well there. I do not think that I have ever seen a gentleman show such obvious interest in a lady after only a few minutes of introduction!"

The heat in her cheeks decided to drop to her throat and then spread out across her chest as Julia looked down at her hands. It had been somewhat disconcerting to realize that she had liked the way Lord Rushington had been smiling at her. If she were to make this endeavor work, then she would have to make certain that she held strong against such reactions.

"Yes, I will admit to being a little flirtatious, but it was not simply to have him smile at me. I think..." Hearing the callousness of her words before she had even spoken them, Julia tried to find another way to explain herself. "He is a gentleman who is, I think, uncaring and heedless of the injury he has caused others. He almost knocked me to the ground as I was on my way to be presented to the Queen and did not *once* come to speak with me. I have not received a single word of apology since then. Now, after the incident at Almack's, I think it is high time that Lord Rushington be treated in much the same way as he treats others."

Instead of gasping with surprise, or frowning hard in obvious displeasure, Miss Glover simply sat there. After a few moments, she nodded.

"I see." Her head tipped to the left. "And what is it that you intend to do?"

The intention she now had was not one she had given a great deal of consideration to, these last few weeks, nor had she lain awake at night and concocted a plan for revenge. Instead, this thought had come to her simply as she had talked with Lord Rushington and had seen his response to her. The way that his lips had curved, sending a flash of interest across his features, had offered her one solution to her current predicament – and she had clung to it.

"I am going to seek my revenge." The words sounded crass and cutting, but she did not hold herself back from them. "Lord Rushington has taken a great deal from me. Aside from you, I have no one else to consider a friend."

"That is because I do not permit society whispers to dictate my actions," Miss Glover interjected, firmly. "*And* because I consider you a friend. I was relieved to hear the truth from you, of course, but even if it had been as Rushington claimed when he railed at you, I would not have turned away from you, nor given you the cut direct, as so many have done. My mother could not persuade me!"

Julia winced, thankful that she had a friend, but at the same time, sorrowful that Lady Westfield now believed the stories about Julia and Lord Rushington.

"You are very kind, and I am truly grateful to you for your friendship. As I have said, Lord Rushington's actions have pushed me back into the corner, have left me set apart from the others, and forced me to become a wallflower. It is not a position I am grateful for, nor one which I want to cling to."

"So, what are you to do?"

Julia took a deep breath.

"I am going to make Lord Rushington fall in love with a wallflower," she stated, firmly.

Miss Glover stared at her.

"And how shall you do that?"

"With flirtations and teasing and a great deal of flattery." Julia's stomach began to twist as she considered precisely how one made someone fall in love. "I will have to do so carefully, since society is, at present, pushing me away from them. However, once he declares himself, I shall declare *myself* and tell him the truth about who I am, and what he has done to me. There will be no happiness for him, just as I have felt no happiness either. What he has taken from me – contentment, excitement, hope – I shall take away from him." Seeing Miss Glover's eyes dart away and the edge of her lip catch between her teeth, Julia let out a slow breath. "I am sorry if you think it a little harsh of me. I do not want to be cruel, but it seems that this gentleman has behaved without consideration for far too long – and now he has truly injured me, in a way that I cannot be saved from."

Miss Glover took a moment, then looked straight back into Julia's eyes.

"I can understand why you feel the need to punish him in such a way," she replied, speaking each word carefully.

"But I would beg of you to be careful. This may be a harsher punishment than you can imagine."

Julia frowned.

"What do you mean?"

It took Miss Glover a few seconds to answer.

"I do not know what it is to be in love." Her eyes softened as she looked across the park and gestured to a gentleman and a lady who were walking together. "I see some ladies who are contented simply to be with a suitable husband, but some who wish for more. I am quite determined to seek a love match, as I may have said before, but I can imagine that to offer one's heart and, thereafter, to find your heart broken and ruined with pain and sorrow must be greatly distressing indeed." Her shoulders lifted and then fell. "It is not something which I should like to experience. I think that it must be one of the greatest pains to endure, for whilst there is no outward injury, no wound which can be attended to or cared for, the agony of a broken heart is still within oneself, and can cause all manner of distress."

Julia nodded slowly, aware of the curl of guilt that wrapped around her heart, urging her to make a different decision – but it was something she shook off quickly.

"You speak as though you *have* experienced it."

"I have not," came the reply. "But one of my dear friends, someone who was wed last Season, endured such pain. She is now wed to a gentleman she did not care for in the least because the one she loved decided that he did not care for her as she cared for him. I am sorrowful for all that she suffered and, whilst I believe that she is as happy and as content as she can be, now, it is a situation which I would beg of you to be careful of encouraging. I understand all that Lord Rushington has done, and can see why the consequences are so distressing, but all the same, I would caution you here."

Looking away, and ignoring the plea of her heart to listen to Miss Glover, Julia took a slow breath and then let it out again, her mind steadfast in its refusal to release such an idea.

"It is the only thing I can think to do," she said after some minutes of silence had passed between them. "The consequences he has placed upon me are very great, and his lack of consideration thereafter only adds to my suffering. How is such a fellow to understand the depths of it, if he too is not permitted to suffer consequences that are placed upon him by another?" The question was left unanswered, and when Miss Glover rose to step away, Julia joined her quickly, but not without sensing the strain that had suddenly formed between them. "You will help me, will you not?"

The question whispered across the wind towards Miss Glover and Julia bit her lip. If Miss Glover did not aid her, then her plans would come to naught. There was no one else she could go to for assistance, no one else who might be willing to step forward.

Miss Glover bit her lip, pausing in her walk to look directly at Julia.

"It is against my better judgment but yes, I will help you." Her long sigh reached Julia, whose heart did not leap with relief but rather shrank a little. "I do not know precisely what you intend to do, but I will stand alongside you regardless. Perhaps I am wrong. Perhaps I ought not to be so eager to pull you back from this. After all, I am not the one who is now nothing but a wallflower."

The words were spoken softly and, whilst Julia was quite certain that they were not meant to injure her, they struck at her with a good deal of strength regardless. Yes, that was what she was now. No one came to converse with her, no gentlemen came to seek out her dance card. Invitations had lessened significantly, and whilst she was no longer the first name on all of society's lips, she was slowly becoming insignificant and forgotten. Yes, she dressed in her finery and made certain to look the very best that she could, but that did nothing to change how she was seen by the *ton*. She adorned the walls now, nothing more than a decorative piece that held no substance within itself but was merely there for people to pass their glances over before continuing on their way.

The guilt evaporated in an instant as her hands curled tight. This was all Lord Rushington's doing. He had mistaken her for someone else and, even though she had no doubt now that he had realized his error, he had done nothing about the matter. When he had looked into her eyes, smiled, and laughed with her, she had seen the lack of consideration in his voice and expression. It was as though nothing hindered him, nothing brought him even a flicker of concern.

What he had done meant nothing. She was the one who would bear the consequences of his foolishness whilst he continued to enjoy society's company without concern.

Something had to be done. Lord Rushington's actions warranted the consequences she would bring upon him. Lifting her chin, Julia took a long breath and set her shoulders, a fresh determination filling her. If she could, she would make Lord Rushington think only of her, his heart yearning for her company, for her embrace... and then she would take it all from him and leave him with a shattered heart.

And it would be just as he deserved.

CHAPTER NINE

The sun was already falling low in the sky as Benedict's carriage approached the Vauxhall Gardens. It was nothing but foolishness to feel any sort of anticipation or excitement, and yet those two emotions tied their hands together and danced a jig all through him. Benedict scowled, running one hand over his chin as he looked steadfastly out of the window.

I still cannot recall her name.

The mysterious young lady would be disappointed this evening when he met her, for he could not readily give her the name that she had been hoping that he would recall. Try as he might, there had been no moment of sudden remembrance, no thrill of delight as he remembered what Miss Glover had called her.

Despite that, however, he was still looking forward to seeing the lady again.

Which is more than ridiculous, given all that I have just experienced with Miss Davenport.

That thought was a sobering one. When it came to Miss Davenport, and how he had been treated by her, he had made a foolish mistake. Having believed himself in love, he had been almost torn apart when he had seen her in the arms of another gentleman, though it was rather interesting to note how quickly he had been pieced back together. There had not been a deep and unsettling grief within him, no sorrow which had been too great to bear. He had not felt the need to drown in his sadness, to sit long by himself and bring her face constantly to mind. No, in coming back to London, he had been able to quickly remove all sorrow from himself and instead was almost happy to be back with his friends. Lord Burnley's company was an excellent aid in that, he supposed, allowing himself a small smile as he recalled the foolishness which they had enjoyed the previous evening.

It had caused no one any harm, of course. Benedict had made a nonchalant remark about how he was quite certain that no gentleman could fill his dance card with the names of ladies of a certain standing and, as he ought to have expected, Lord Burnley had immediately said he would do so and prove Benedict wrong. Benedict had taken on the challenge with him and thus, they had together sought out only the daughters of Earls, Marquesses, or Dukes to dance with. It had been a very difficult task, for he had to either make certain that he was acquainted with the ladies he spoke to or find a way to have himself introduced to them before he could ask for their dance card – though he had achieved what he had set out to do. Lord Burnley had been quite certain of his success also, until another of their friends, Lord Gregson, had pointed out that a particular lady was not the daughter of an Earl as Lord Burnley had believed, but the daughter of a Viscount. Lord Burnley had been so very angry at this discovery that he had left the ball entirely, though he had made his peace with Benedict over a glass of whisky at White's in the hours thereafter.

It was all nonsense, but it was very pleasant nonsense, and Benedict found enjoyment in that... though what this evening might bring in comparison, he could not yet say.

Alighting from the carriage, he made his way to the entrance and stood for a moment, looking out at the park and the many visitors already within it. There was a beauty about this place that was like no other, and his smile lifted at the thought of sharing it with the mysterious young lady whose eyes had lit up when he'd described the place.

If only I could remember her name.

"Good evening, Lord Rushington."

As if she had been waiting for him to think of her, the young lady in question drew near, with Miss Glover and her mother a few steps behind. She dropped into a curtsey, and Benedict bowed quickly, allowing a smile to dance across his face when she lifted one eyebrow in obvious question.

"No, my dear lady, I confess my foolishness, and state that I do not recall your name. I have done my utmost to think of it, to recall a moment when your title was given to me, but I think, in my delight at your company and our conversation, I have quite forgotten it."

Her eyes twinkled, but she pulled out her fan and let it hide her smile from him, her gaze searching his features as if she wanted to make certain that he spoke the truth.

"Very well. Then you may call me Miss Smith."

"Miss Smith?" That was clearly *not* her name, but one which was so very common, particularly amongst the lower classes, that it would not distinguish her from any other. "You are not to give me your true title, then?"

"That is to be your consequence, Lord Rushington." Her fan slipped away but her smile, to his surprise, was a little cool. Had he truly disappointed her with his lack of recall? "You shall not know me as I truly am, not until you are able to earn my favor."

He bowed again, accepting what she had said with a hint of concern beginning to build within him.

"Very well, if that is what you require. And what shall I do to garner your favor?"

This time, when she smiled, it spread a fresh brightness across her features and Benedict allowed himself a small breath of relief. It was strange how much her opinion meant to him, he considered, a little surprised that he had been so affected by her upset.

"You might begin by offering me your arm, Lord Rushington. I do have high expectations for this evening. and I hope that everything is as good as you have described it to be."

Offering his arm at once, he quickly greeted Miss Glover and her mother before turning himself back towards the Vauxhall Gardens.

"The Gardens are truly magnificent, I assure you," he promised her, looking down at her and wishing that her bonnet did not hide so much of her features. "You shall see sights which are unlike anything you have ever seen before. Of that, you can be quite certain."

"That sounds rather thrilling." She glanced up at him and then looked away again. "I confess to having very little excitement in my life at present, so this is sure to be exhilarating."

The remark caused Benedict to frown, though he did not ask her anything. If she was closely acquainted with Miss Glover, then he presumed their ages to be around the same. Perhaps this was her second Season? He could not tell without asking her, and that was not something that he wished to do at present but, all the same, he did wonder about her statement and what it might mean. Was it that she did not enjoy the Season? Was she restricted in some way? Perhaps her father was very stern and held her back from what she wished very much to do but, if that was the situation, then he was a little surprised that she had been permitted to go to Vauxhall Gardens.

"You are frowning, Lord Rushington. Have I displeased you in some way?"

The light teasing in her voice had him grinning at her, pleased to know that she had been watching him.

"Not in the least. I was only thinking about your last remark."

"Oh."

Her eyes caught his again and then fell away.

"I do hope that this evening will bring you some of the excitement which you have been lacking thus far," he continued, warmly. "There now, you see? We come to it. What do you think of the sight, Miss Smith? Is it not magnificent?"

Miss Smith did not take another step. Benedict frowned at once, the smile falling away from his face only to let his gaze fix itself to her features. Upon seeing her astonishment, the flickering lamps burning in her wide eyes and the soft circle of her lips, Benedict smiled softly and said nothing more, glancing over his shoulder to see Miss Glover and her mother gazing out at the sight also.

Vauxhall Gardens were utterly magnificent and Benedict himself cast an appreciative eye over them. There were many walks that they might take together and, within those walks, the ground and trees would be lit with colored lamps as well as other decorative pieces.

"It is... enchanting."

Miss Smith's eyes were still very round indeed, but Benedict smiled into them, having dropped her arm and come around a little more to face her.

"I am delighted to hear you say so. Why do we not go in together? There is so much that I should like to show you."

Miss Smith nodded but did not pull her gaze away from the grounds to look back into his face. Rather than being frustrated by this, Benedict only smiled. Being in company with Miss Smith was proving rather delightful and, as he took her arm again, Benedict's spirits lifted all the more. It was not the Gardens which thrilled him so, he realized, but rather the company he now kept. For some inexplicable reason, Miss Smith's delight and surprise at seeing the Gardens was filling his heart with so much happiness and contentment, he did not think he would be able to stop smiling for the rest of the evening.

~

"What did you think of that performance?"

Benedict leaned in towards Miss Smith, catching a hint of roses as she turned her head towards him. The scent ran down into the pit of his stomach and turned itself into a small pool of desire, forcing him to lean away from her again.

"I thought it…" Miss Smith turned her head back to his, searching his face while the edge of her lip was caught gently between her teeth. "The truth is, Lord Rushington, I do not know *what* I would say to that. It is utterly extraordinary! I have never before seen a tightrope walker and to see her do such a thing as that was both exhilarating and terrifying!"

"I quite agree." Benedict chuckled when Miss Smith's

smile brought a hint of color to her cheeks. "Madame Saqui is quite extraordinary. I do believe that she is one of the Garden's very best attractions."

"Though there is still the fireworks display," Miss Glover put in, coming to stand beside Miss Smith and smiling at him, though her smile did not reach her eyes and faded a little too quickly to be truly genuine. "Although I must say that I was most impressed at Madame Saqui's skill." Looking over her shoulder, she gestured to where her mother was in conversation with another lady. "I said to Mama that, should I find no one suitable to marry, I shall come to join the circus here at Vauxhall Gardens and be very happy indeed."

"Until you fall and break your head," Miss Smith answered before Benedict could speak, nudging her friend who immediately broke into laughter. "No, I think that, on my part, I shall be more than contented coming to watch the circus from time to time."

"I should be glad to accompany you again."

Miss Glover melted away as he said this, leaving him and Miss Smith to speak alone. Benedict's heart had leaped up as he had spoken those words, but he did not immediately try to pull them back, not at all regretting what he had said. He was enjoying Miss Smith's company, even though he found her unwillingness to tell him her true title to be a little infuriating – though that was entirely his own fault, he supposed.

"That is very kind of you, Lord Rushington."

This was not an acceptance of his offer, Benedict realized, and frowning, he took a small step closer to her, dropping his voice low.

"Would you have no desire to return here? Or would you prefer not to step out with me?"

Instantly, Miss Smith's green eyes rounded a little as if she were uncertain as to how to respond.

"Pray do not think that I..." Trailing off, she closed her eyes momentarily. "Yes, I should be very glad to step out with you again." Her smile returned quickly, and her gaze returned to his face. "I am a little overwhelmed, that is all."

"The Vauxhall Gardens are inclined to induce such feelings, I think," he told her, with a smile. "Come now. Miss Glover is quite correct, the fireworks are still to come, and I think that those shall overwhelm you even more!"

Her hand went to his arm before he even had a chance to offer it.

"So long as you are there, ready to support me, then all shall be well, I am sure."

The gentle purr of her voice had his eyes flaring in surprise, a breath hitching in his chest as he looked back at her. For a moment, he saw Miss Davenport looking back at him, only then realizing the soft similarities between their features – the same green eyes, oval lips, and rosebud mouth – only to see that Miss Smith was vastly different from Miss Davenport in so many ways. Her smile was sweeter, eyes holding fast to his rather than darting away as Miss Davenport's had so often done.

Walking with her along the path toward the viewing area for the fireworks, an unsettling feeling began to wind its way into Benedict's happiness, twisting through it and, little by little, breaking it apart. In seeing a few similarities to Miss Davenport in Miss Smith's features, he had now brought the former back to mind. Only a few weeks ago, he had proposed to the lady, and she had accepted, only for her to reveal her true self and break apart from him entirely. Was he now in danger of allowing himself to become caught up with another young lady? The only reason he had returned to London was to seek out enjoyment and laughter, rather than in the hope of finding another young lady whom he might give his attentions to.

So what, precisely, was he doing now?

He had only just asked Miss Smith if she would like to step out with him again and, given that she had accepted, he now had no other choice but to do precisely that.

But the more time I spend with the lady, the more intrigued I am with her.

Gritting his teeth, Benedict resisted the urge to sigh aloud, knowing that it would cause Miss Smith to look at him and wonder what it was that he felt at the present moment. Was he allowing himself to become taken up with another young lady, despite his intention *not* to do so? Or was there something about Miss Smith that truly interested him, genuinely pulled him towards her? And if there was, then what was that going to mean for his heart?

CHAPTER TEN

"Another meeting with Lord Rushington?"

Julia nodded and set down her teacup on the china plate.

"Yes, it is to be our fourth, I think. After the first, I came across him near the milliner's, though I only had my maid. Given it was raining, we stepped into the shop and spoke briefly." Her hand lifted as she ticked off the occasions. "We next met in the London library the following day, though I think he was there by design since I had spoken to him of my intentions."

"I see."

Miss Glover sipped her tea before nodding slowly, her gaze vague as she looked around the room. Julia waited for her friend to say something more but, as silence spun its web across the room, she realized that Miss Glover had nothing more she wished to express at that moment.

"I have had to take great care thus far," she found herself saying, simply to break the silence. "Our second meeting at Vauxhall Gardens went very well as it was at the

Gardens and, therefore, under the cover of darkness – albeit broken by the sheer number of lights and the fireworks – but it was enough for no one else to recognize me. It was raining when we met at the milliner's and the London library is very quiet indeed, so no one threw a look at me or gave me the cut direct. That might have brought with it a good number of questions."

"Which you are understandably loath to answer." Miss Glover smiled, no harshness in her words. "I must say, I was a little surprised to see how quickly Lord Rushington has responded to you." Julia's eyes flared, only for Miss Glover to begin spluttering, her tea quickly set down on the table and one hand gesticulating wildly. "That is not what I meant, I assure you. It is not that I think you poor in beauty or in character but rather -"

"I shall take no offense." Managing a smile, Julia sat back in her chair a little more, the sting of her friend's words dancing across her skin even though she understood it had not been meant with any cruelty. "You mean to say that you think it surprising, because of what he shared with Miss Davenport?"

"Precisely." Miss Glover's face had gone a little white, though her shoulders dropped a little, free of the tension that had gripped her only a few moments ago. "For a gentleman who was betrothed a little over a month ago to now be showing so much of an interest in another is somewhat surprising. I would not have said so, had I not believed that he had a great depth of feeling for Miss Davenport."

Julia nodded slowly and picked up her tea again.

"I suppose that is something which cannot be denied."

"No, it cannot. A gentleman who spoke as he did to you, albeit in the belief that you were Miss Davenport, must have had a heart filled with great and heavy emotions about the lady." Miss Glover tilted her head. "But they appear to have faded very quickly indeed, given the interest he is showing in you. *That* is where my surprise comes from."

"Mayhap I am nothing more than a distraction from his broken heart." Julia shrugged. "Regardless of the reason, I am grateful for the eagerness he seems to be expressing for my company. That is exactly what I want."

"You certainly have intrigued him!" Miss Glover laughed softly and tilted her head. "And where are you to meet him this afternoon?"

"We are to take a walk in St James' Park." Julia bit her lip, a little nervous. "I have not told my mother about the arrangement, however. I shall ask to take the carriage for a short drive around London and will take my maid also. I will not inform them about who I am meeting, however."

It cast a shadow over her heart to keep the truth from her mother, but there was nothing else to be done. If she was to tell Lady Harbison about what was taking place, she would then be forced into a long and full explanation about what she was doing, and her intentions behind it, also. For the moment, it was best to try to do what she could to avoid her mother's questions.

"I should be able to join you if you wish, though I promise to stay far behind." Miss Glover lifted one shoulder and then let it fall. "I have a few afternoon callers, but no one of any importance. If I take tea with them briefly and then step out thereafter, my mother will not be able to complain!"

Julia smiled at her friend.

"You would be willing to do so? I can write to Lord Rushington so that he is aware of it."

"I would." Miss Glover let out a small sigh and put out her hands on either side, her shoulders lifting a little. "I am concerned for you, I confess."

"Concerned?" A little surprised, Julia lifted her eyebrows high. "In what respect?"

"I am concerned that you will find yourself completely and utterly in love with Lord Rushington."

Miss Glover spoke with such bluntness that her words kicked Julia in the chest, her breath rushing from her lungs.

"I – I can assure you, I –"

"That is precisely the point. You cannot assure me of anything," Miss Glover interrupted, firmly. "You have a gentleman of quality who regards you as though he has never before seen the sunshine on a beautiful warm day. Yes, it may be because he is a little confused over the mystery which you have presented him with, of your name, but that does not mean that his interest is not genuine. If it is, and if he grows closer to you, in a way that no gentleman has done before, then how, precisely, will you respond, Julia?"

The question was not one that Julia could answer. Her mouth went dry, and she looked away, turning her gaze to the window as though something there would provide her with the answer she was looking for.

"I am determined."

It was not an answer, but rather a statement, making it clear to both herself and her friend that she would not permit herself to be distracted from her task by any gentleman's desires.

Miss Glover let out a slow breath but shook her head as she did so.

"I am certain that you are, my dear friend," she said, quietly, "but determination can fade. Feelings can change.

Resolutions wash away. *That* is why I tell you that I am concerned. There is always the chance that what you desire from Lord Rushington – for him to fall in love with you – might turn into a situation where you both come to care for each other. And in that circumstance, I think it would be very difficult for you – perhaps even impossible - to turn around and state that you do *not* care for him. If you find your heart filled with him, will you truly have the strength to break *his* heart into pieces?"

Julia tossed her head, refusing to allow Miss Glover's questions to have any impact on her whatsoever.

"I can assure you, Mary, I will not allow myself to fall in love with him," she stated firmly. "After what he has done to me after his harsh and cruel actions have pushed me into being a wallflower, can you truly question whether I will permit my heart to feel anything for him?"

Miss Glover gazed back at her steadily before, after some moments, she picked up her tea and sipped it carefully, saying nothing more. Julia did the same, trying to push away Miss Glover's questions and telling herself silently that she had no real reason to be concerned. She would not fall in love with Lord Rushington! If she ever had even a *hint* of feeling, all that was required was to bring up the memory of him shouting at her in the middle of the dance floor, his face ugly with anger and upset. She would recall the tears she had wept, the hollow within her as she had realized the depths to which he had allowed her to fall by his inaction thereafter.

No, there was no possible way for her heart to be full of him. Even the idea was foolish and, setting down her teacup, Julia took a deep breath and let her lungs fill, determination pushing its way to the fore again.

"This afternoon, then," she said, as Miss Glover

nodded, her eyes still filled with questions that Julia had no intention of answering. "St James' Park?" Giving her friend the time and the place, she smiled as Miss Glover confirmed that yes, she would be present also. "I thank you."

"Of course. And please, Julia," Miss Glover finished, leaning forward in her chair just a little. "Please do be careful."

I DO NOT KNOW what Mary is concerned about.

Seeing Lord Rushington's carriage arrive, Julia made her way forward, alongside Miss Glover and her maid. Julia's carriage was parked at the other end of the park, ready for them once the walk with Lord Rushington was completed.

I am certain that I will not give my heart to him. This is meant to be a punishment, a consequence for the pain and suffering which he has placed upon me. I would be a fool to –

"Good afternoon, Miss Glover, and to you also, Miss Smith." Lord Rushington bowed. "How glad I am to see you again."

Her thoughts were cut into pieces and flung to different parts of the park as Lord Rushington inclined his head, his hat in one hand. When he looked at her, his blue eyes clear and matching the sky above them, his smile warm, and his dark hair gleaming gently in the sunshine, she found all thoughts suddenly stolen away from her. With a tight swirl of breath in her chest, she barely managed to complete her curtsey, wobbling slightly as she rose back to standing.

How very odd.

"Good afternoon, Lord Rushington. Might I ask if you have recalled my name?"

Lord Rushington chuckled.

"Am I to be greeted this way every time we meet, Miss Smith?"

"I take it from that, then, that you have not?" Her smile curved gently though her stomach cramped inexplicably at the same time. "I fear that you shall soon go and ask one of your friends and then I shall lose my power over you!"

With a laugh that seemed to fill the air around her with light, Lord Rushington shook his head and smiled.

"I do not think that any of them would be able to aid me with this, Miss Smith, even if I should go to ask them. After all, you tend to stay away from society gatherings, from what I have seen." A gentle lift to his eyebrow told her that there was a question within that statement, and she hesitated, wondering how she would explain her absence from society.

"Shall we begin to walk?" said Miss Glover. And so Julia did not have to answer his question.

Lord Rushington agreed, and they soon fell into step together, though it did not take more than ten steps for Miss Glover to begin to fall behind, leaving Julia and Lord Rushington to their conversation. Julia glanced behind her at her friend, but Miss Glover only smiled, sending an inexplicable flush into Julia's cheeks as she looked up at Lord Rushington. He too was smiling, though his eyes were not fixed to hers. Was he enjoying their time together? Or was he thinking of some other matter which was now setting such happiness across his face? "You are somewhat mysterious, Miss Smith." Julia blinked, a little taken aback by his sudden statement. "First of all, you will not remind me of your name and thereafter, I soon discover that you are not to be found at any social events."

Trying to ignore the whisper of warning in her mind,

Julia placed her hand on his arm for a brief moment, causing him to look sharply up at her.

"Do you mean to say that you have been looking for me?"

"Of course I have!" The exclamation was so great that it caused Julia's heart to flutter in surprise. "You cannot think that I *like* being unaware of a lady's name, Miss Smith! It is something of an embarrassment to find myself so flummoxed, to know that I ought to have been paying attention but, instead, became so distracted by the beauty presented to me, I could not take note as I should have." This heady compliment had Julia's stomach rising so high, it was as if it wanted to lodge itself in her throat. She did not know what to make of such a remark. Was he truly being sincere? Did he truly think her beautiful? "Your silence is noted, Miss Smith but I warn you..." Trailing off, he reached for her hand and settled it upon his arm, grinning at her with flashes of darkness in his blue eyes. "I usually give all that I can into getting what I desire."

Julia's heart thrummed and she looked away, tingling running down to the very tips of her fingers. Whilst her plan to have Lord Rushington fall in love with her appeared to be going fairly well thus far, she had not expected to have to battle her own emotions because of him. Her response to his smile, his touch, and his nearness held a strength she had not anticipated.

"Ah, you will not put me out of my misery then," Lord Rushington sighed, though his smile lingered despite the heaviness of his breath. "You wish to punish me because of my foolishness."

"Yes, I am afraid that I do," Julia answered, with a fervency that made Lord Rushington laugh, entirely unaware of how strongly she meant it. "You shall have to endure a great deal."

"But it is *most* unfair," Lord Rushington replied, brushing his fingers across hers as they rested on his arm. "You will not tell me, I have not seen you with either your parents, or amongst society, and I cannot ask any of my acquaintances for, as I have said, you are not at social occasions, from what I have seen. I have frequented many during my time in London this Season and I am certain that I have not ever set eyes upon you. And indeed, I have made certain to search for you when I have been at soirees and the like these last few days. It seems to me, Miss Smith, that you are insistent upon keeping yourself hidden away – either that, or you seek out only specific company. Mayhap I ought to be very pleased that you have agreed to spend a little time with me!"

When he laughed, Julia had to grit her teeth and force only the smallest tilt of her lips. In an instant, all that she felt over his closeness to her was washed away as a wave of frustration poured across her soul. Yes, she was hidden away – and it was entirely *his* doing! It was not as though she wanted this, not as if she had decided to keep herself back from society! His actions – and then his inaction thereafter – had made that decision for her. Throwing him a glance, she caught the look in his eyes, the questions which still burned there, and barely managed to smile.

"I confess that I find society to be a little troublesome."

It was all she could think to say, but Lord Rushington seemed to understand. His smile fled, his eyes shuttered, and he looked away quickly. They walked in silence and Julia pressed her lips tightly together. Had there been something in what she had said which had upset him? That was not at all what she wanted.

"Society can be *very* troublesome, I will admit." Lord Rushington broke the quiet, offering her a small but wry smile. "It is not always a friend, though I will state that I have found a good deal of enjoyment also."

Julia nodded but said nothing. What was there that she could say to such a remark?

"I wonder if you, despite your desire to keep yourself a little back from society, have already heard of my particular difficulties?" Scarlet spread itself over his cheeks, but his gaze remained steady. "It was some weeks ago, and gossip has now moved to another matter entirely, but all the same, it was chattered about amongst almost everyone, I am sure."

Licking her lips, Julia looked straight ahead rather than toward him, her mind scrambling over what she ought to say. Should she admit that yes, she knew about Miss Davenport and his ruined betrothal, or should she remain silent?

"You are unwilling to speak of it, I think." Lord Rushington pressed her hand again and let out a slow breath. "I admire you for that, I confess. Gossip and whispers do nothing but cause injury, do they not?"

Again, the wave of frustration crashed over her, leaving embers of burning anger in its wake.

"They do indeed."

The urge to tell him everything, to state precisely what he had done, and how it had injured her, was so great that it took all of her strength of will to keep her lips closed. Lord Rushington stopped their walk, turned to face her, and tipped his head. Somehow, without her even realizing it, he had taken hold of her hand, rather than have her resting it gently on his arm. Sparks began to shoot up towards her heart.

"I shall be the opposite of you, I think." Struggling, with

her feelings pulling her first in one direction, only to then drag her in entirely the opposite direction, Julia could do nothing other than look back into his eyes. "You will remain a mysterious, beautiful creature, whom I shall have to fight to discover, whilst I shall permit myself to be entirely open towards you. There is much about me that, either you do not know, or you pretend not to know, and thus, I shall take great care to speak to you about all that has taken place. I wish to make certain that you understand what I have endured these last few months... and the foolishness of my actions also." A small smile crooked up one side of his mouth. "What say you to that?"

Julia blinked. Was this what she wanted? When she had decided to do her best to have Lord Rushington fall in love with her, she had not given too great a consideration to what that would be like. To her mind, she had assumed it would be a mere case of attempting to be as teasing and as mysterious as she could, but never had she thought that he might then begin to open up to her with any sort of vulnerability. To know him as she thought he was – cruel, inconsiderate, foolish, and reckless was more than enough for her. She needed no more than that – but it seemed that Lord Rushington was determined to provide her more, regardless.

He was waiting for her answer.

"If you say this in the hope that I shall reveal my true name to you, then I am afraid that you will be sadly disappointed." Her voice sounded hollow, thin, and brittle, despite the note of teasing she attempted to place within it. "I will not be moved."

"No, I say it not in the hope of gaining anything in return," he answered softly, his thumb running over the back of her hand. "But simply because I wish to." His shoulders lifted in a shrug. "I cannot explain my desire to be truthful with you in such a way, but there it remains – and I must give way to it." His eyes slid over her shoulder, and he quickly dropped her hand, as if he had only just remembered that Miss Glover was with them. "I only hope that you will not think too poorly of me."

CHAPTER ELEVEN

*B*enedict ran one hand over his chin as he meandered slowly along the path by the river. He was pleased that Miss Smith had agreed to meet with him again, but every time he suggested taking tea or the like, she had always refused. It had been almost three weeks since their first meeting but thus far, he still could not recall her name and, given that he was not able to point her out to any of his friends, did not think that he ever would! Perhaps she would have to continue being called Miss Smith for the rest of her days.

But how can I grow closer to her if I do not know her true title?

"Whatever *can* you be thinking about, Rushington?"

Benedict blinked, then came to a stop, seeing Lord Burnley grinning at him, standing only a short distance away.

"Good afternoon, Burnley."

"Good afternoon. Might I ask where you are going? You have been walking very slowly and appear deep in thought

– though mayhap the thoughts are not as pleasant as you might wish them to be?"

Coming to walk alongside Benedict, he waited with a lifted eyebrow for an answer, though Benedict was not overly inclined to give it.

"I have a specific situation in mind, that is all."

"And what is this situation?"

Benedict shook his head.

"It is a mystery which I must find a way through." Wincing inwardly at the light that immediately filled his friend's eyes, he berated himself silently for saying the very thing that was likely to incite his friend's interest. "Do not ask me the details, for I will not give them to you."

"No? And why ever not?" Lord Burnley's expression instantly lifted into one of surprise, followed by his brows dropping low. "These last two weeks, I have found you increasingly absent, I must admit. I thought your desire to return to London after your sister's wedding was for laughter and ridiculous nonsense, which we *had* only just returned to, only for you to then begin to distance yourself again." There came a slight narrowing of his eyes. "What is it that keeps you away? It is not the matter with that young lady and your confusion over her and Miss Davenport, is it?"

"No, indeed not!" Benedict huffed out a laugh, seeing Lord Burnley nod his relief. "I confess that I have not given that a single thought these last few weeks. After our discussion on the matter, I came to the conclusion that you were right, and I did not need to pursue the issue any longer – and I have not done so. I have not let myself think on it."

"Then what *have* you been thinking about?" Lord Burnley asked, pointedly. "There must be something significant to this mystery that has pulled you away from my company which, if I might say myself, is very often sought out by a good many others! Especially if you will not speak of it to me!"

Chuckling, Benedict rolled his eyes at his friend's teasing arrogance.

"It is of significance, yes," he admitted, quietly, his smile beginning to drift away. "I find myself quite caught up with it."

"Tell me."

Benedict sighed heavily, seeing his friend's frown, and wondering whether or not he ought to say anything. It was not as if Miss Smith had forbidden him from speaking of her to anyone else, but all the same, there was something about what he had with her, the bond of mystery and interest, which he wanted to keep all to himself. His gaze lifted back along the path, only to catch sight of none other than the young lady in question. She was, as he had expected, standing with Miss Glover, their maids a little way behind them both. His heart leaped up suddenly, evidently thrilled to be in her company again, although he kept his features quite fixed so Lord Burnley would not notice.

"Ah, there is Miss Glover." The nonchalance with which he spoke was heavily affected but thankfully, Lord Burnley did not seem to notice. "Are you acquainted with the lady?"

"I am." Lord Burnley threw him a look then returned it to Miss Glover. "I do not think I have ever come across a young lady who speaks as much as she!"

"I admit to finding her a pleasure to talk with," Benedict replied, earning him a look of surprise from his friend. "Although I am not yet acquainted with the young lady beside her."

Lord Burnley gave her only a passing glance, then shrugged.

"I do not know her either," he said, before continuing on his way, leaving Benedict to wonder what he was to do.

He could not simply walk past Miss Smith but at the same time, did not want to expose his lie to Lord Burnley. He had only just stated that he was not acquainted with her, and could not now go to her side only for her to state to Lord Burnley that yes, they were already known to each other.

"You have not told me why *you* are walking here," Benedict said hastily, wondering if he might distract Lord Burnley from his walk. "Did you think only to stop and wait for me?"

Lord Burnley chuckled and stopped, looking back at Benedict.

"No, I am to meet with Lord Henderson... and his sister. Apparently, the lady is a beauty and I confess, I am rather intrigued when it comes to beauty."

Benedict grinned.

"Very well. I think I shall speak with Miss Glover and her companion for a few moments so that they do not think us both rude for walking past them!"

Lord Burnley narrowed his eyes immediately, telling Benedict that there was an immediate suspicion over such an action. Choosing to remain as unperturbed as he could, Benedict said nothing more, keeping his stance relaxed and his smile pinned to his face. After some moments, Lord Burnley shrugged and turned away, and Benedict let out a silent breath of relief. He watched Lord Burnley for a few more seconds, making certain that his friend did not turn around and come marching back immediately, before finally, making his way back towards Miss Smith and Miss Glover.

"Good afternoon."

"Good afternoon, Lord Rushington. I thought you were to walk past us!" Miss Smith smiled though her green eyes held a myriad of questions, each swirling gently. "Was that a friend of yours?"

"Yes, that was Lord Burnley." Benedict glanced to his left, a twist of concern filling him as if he expected Lord Burnley to jump out at any moment. "He is gone to meet with another gentleman."

"And you did not think to introduce us?" There was a note of gentle teasing in Miss Glover's voice, though she put one hand to her hip. "We might have been glad of another acquaintance."

"I thought it best not to do so. After all, I would not want to use my friend to recall Miss Smith's true title!"

It was a thin excuse and Benedict looked to Miss Smith, a little concerned that she felt the same way as her friend, only to see her smiling gently, clearly pleased with his response.

"How very considerate and honest of you, Lord Rushington."

"I am glad that you think so."

When Benedict put out his arm, Miss Smith took it at once, sending a smile to Miss Glover who quickly nodded in clear understanding. A small trail of heat ran up his spine at the look the two ladies shared. They were both all too aware that he desired to walk and converse with Miss Smith and she seemed more than contented with the situation, such as it was... so why then did he suddenly feel so ill at ease?

Frowning, he resisted the urge to rub one hand over his forehead. The last time he had spoken with Miss Smith, he had stated his intention to be as open and as honest with her as he could. Part of such a statement had come with the hope that should he say such a thing – and do as he had stated – she might then be willing to allow him a little more into her sphere. The other part of his intention had been to simply be clear as to what had occurred with Miss Davenport. It was not something that he could fully explain, but the more time he spent with Miss Smith, the more he wanted to be truthful with her about what he had endured, and the foolishness of his own actions also. There was very little doubt in his mind that she was already aware of something, given the rumors and whispers that had been flying about London in his absence, and that awareness was what drove him.

"The day is lovely, I think." Miss Smith's head turned towards him, a small sigh escaping from her lips. "Do you not think so, Lord Rushington?"

"I do." The tension in his frame began to slowly fade as he walked alongside her, all too aware that the desire within himself to be honest with her was growing all the more. "When last we spoke, there was in that discussion an acknowledgment of some whispers about me which you neither acknowledged nor denied knowing."

Miss Smith's lips quirked.

"And I shall continue to do the same, I am afraid."

"And that is entirely your prerogative," he agreed, smiling at her. "But I wish to inform you of what took place." The smile began to dim as he recalled the night when he had betrothed himself to Miss Davenport, only to find his heart torn asunder but a short while later. How strange it was to realize that there was not so much as a bruise still lingering there! "I want to make myself plain, Miss Smith, so nothing is hidden from you."

"You seem to care about my consideration of you, Lord Rushington."

"Indeed, I do." He did not hesitate as he responded, a fresh fervency in his voice which he did not even attempt to hide. "Which is why I must tell you that I have been a very foolish fellow." This was met with a small exclamation of surprise as Miss Smith turned her head to look directly at him, her eyes a little more rounded than before. "I was," Benedict said again, very firmly indeed. "I am a gentleman who has always been inclined towards a little frivolity, and certainly some foolishness over the London Season, but never before have I permitted myself to behave in a way such as this!" Shaking his head to himself, he continued before she had a chance to interject. "I met a young lady and thought her the most wonderful creature in all the world. After only the briefest of acquaintances, I decided that I must be in love with her and continued to pursue her as best I could."

"I see."

Miss Smith's voice was very faint, and Benedict glanced at her, aware of the lines which now formed across her forehead.

"I was not in love with her." The words came easily enough, and Benedict caught himself nodding, beginning to realize the truth now. "I believed that I was, but even my own sister warned me to be cautious. She reminded me that I had not had even the opportunity to have a prolonged conversation with the lady in question, and had not spent a great deal of time in her company, but I did not believe that to be of any concern."

Miss Smith coughed quietly, then pressed his arm gently.

"And might I ask why you could not spend longer in her

company? If you believed yourself to be in love, then–"

"Because she was already being courted by another." Catching the quick intake of breath, Benedict winced visibly. "And thus, the story of my foolishness continues."

"I see."

Miss Smith was blinking rapidly, her gaze away from him now.

"Another gentleman had asked to court her and had been accepted," Benedict continued, speaking quickly so he might finish the story as soon as possible. "And yet, I was singularly determined to make her my bride."

At this, Miss Smith stopped walking, her hand loosening from his arm as she turned to look at him.

"You proposed? Whilst she was being courted by another gentleman?"

The tone of her voice left him in no doubt what it was that she thought of such behavior, and Benedict was quick to correct her.

"No, she was no longer being courted by Lord Thomlinson when I proposed, Miss Smith, though I will admit to being more than a little obvious when it came to expressing my desires. Miss Davenport knew what I wished for, understood my longings, and told me, much to my gratification, that she felt the same way. The only reason she had accepted Lord Thomlinson was her father's urging, but she had no true feelings for him. Thus, she begged me to wait until she could find a way to make sure that the connection between herself and Lord Thomlinson came to a close in a proper manner – and thus, I waited. My sister was quite correct, however. By this point, I had not spent a great deal of time in her company, nor had I enjoyed more than one or two very brief conversations with her, but I was still more than convinced that I was in love with the lady. Looking back upon that, hearing myself say such things, I confess to being very foolish indeed. I proposed to a young lady whose character I did not know, but whose face was the only thing I had truly considered. Convincing myself that her character would match her outward beauty, when she told me matters were at an end between herself and Lord Thomlinson, I practically leaped at her. I proposed at almost the very same moment, and while you will think me a buffoon for doing so – and I will admit I was, also – she accepted me."

"So, you were betrothed." She began to move, and Benedict fell into step beside Miss Smith, walking with her again, now that her initial shock was at an end. "But no longer, I presume."

"No, indeed not!" Benedict managed to chuckle, though the sound faded quickly. "Now that I think about it, now that I understand the truth for what it is, I see that the very reason Lord Thomlinson ended his courtship is the very same as the reason that broke our betrothal asunder."

"Oh?"

Her eyes found his again, searching them gently.

"She told me that Lord Thomlinson disapproved of the company she kept. I do not know what such company was, however, but if it was the same company which *I* saw her in, then I can understand his displeasure." When Miss Smith's eyebrows rose, Benedict sighed heavily and explained himself. "Once we were betrothed, I was overwhelmed with delight. I am sure you can imagine, therefore, the depths of despair I found myself flung into when I watched her step into the arms of another gentleman. She did not know that I was watching her, of course, which made matters all the worse."

"Oh, I am sorry." Miss Smith's hand made its way back

to his arm, a gentle sympathy in her tone. "That must have been profoundly difficult."

"It was – but strangely, I am glad of it. It is because of what I witnessed that the betrothal between myself and Miss Davenport came to an end. I do not tell you this for you to think ill of her, Miss Smith, but rather so that you might think ill of *me*."

Miss Smith stopped once more though her hand did not pull away as she looked up into his face, her eyes a little rounded.

"I do not understand. You want me to think poorly of you?"

"I do not *want* it, but I expect it," Benedict answered, quietly. "I will confess to you that I find that my desire for your company grows ever stronger, but I wish, at the same time, to be entirely honest about the mistakes and foolishness in which I have involved myself. Knowing that you would have heard rumors and the like, I think it is only fair to be truthful with you. I thought myself in love with Miss Davenport, and she proved me to be a fool, but I have learned from what I suffered. I have recognized my haste and my overeager heart, and I am determined not to behave in such a manner again."

Miss Smith remained quiet for some minutes. They walked together, her hand on his arm, their steps slow, and both minds, no doubt, considering what had been said. Benedict clamped his lips shut, refusing to permit himself to say one word more, even though the silence from Miss Smith was difficult to endure. He wondered what it was that she was thinking of him, what it was that she was considering. There was the chance that she might choose to step back from him, to end their connection over his past foolishness and, if that was what she was to do, then Benedict would have no choice but to accept it – even if he did not wish for it. Ice flooded his heart and he shivered violently, only for Miss Smith to look up at him.

"Miss Davenport, is she...?"

"She is betrothed and preparing for her wedding day." Understanding what it was that she had been thinking to ask him, Benedict managed a smile. "I do not have even a single modicum of feeling remaining when it comes to Miss Davenport, I assure you. It is as though, in being freed from her, I have realized the ridiculousness of my actions – though I did not feel this way immediately, I confess it! I was angry – furious, in fact – and broken-hearted." Allowing himself a shrug, he glanced at her again. "Now, however, I confess to being a little relieved to have been saved from what, to my mind, would have been an utterly disastrous connection."

"Thank you for explaining all to me." Miss Smith took a deep breath and lifted her chin, but gazed straight ahead, not looking at him. "You are very good to be so truthful."

"It is because I want to be," he answered, truthfully. "I do not want there to be confusion or whispers of rumors between us. I wish to be honest."

"And so you have been." The strength in Miss Smith's voice faded to almost a whisper as she finally turned her head to look at him again. "And mayhap I will join you in that." With another breath, she squeezed her eyes closed for a moment, her face a little paler now, even with the sunshine and the warmth of the afternoon. "My name, Lord Rushington. I think I shall share it with you."

Benedict came to an immediate stop, twisting sharply towards her.

"You have no need to, Miss Smith, not unless you truly

wish to. I am contented to call you Miss Smith, rather than your true title, until I recall your name."

Her smile lifted briefly, though her eyes did not flash with light.

"You shall never recall it, Lord Rushington, for I did not give it to you. Not once."

A cold shiver ran down his frame.

"Why not?"

"Because I enjoyed teasing you."

It was an answer that took some of his confusion away. He did not find any anger growing because of her statement, but instead found his smile lifting just a little

"I see."

"Miss Smith?"

The quiet voice of Miss Glover broke through their conversation, and stole the moment away, leaving Benedict with a sharp pain stabbing through his chest. Miss Smith had been on the cusp of revealing her name, a name which he now understood he had never heard before.

"We should return to the carriage. We do not have very long."

Miss Smith nodded then looked back to Benedict.

"Forgive me, Lord Rushington." Her eyes glinted gently. "It appears as though my truth shall have to wait a little while longer."

CHAPTER TWELVE

I came so close to telling him the truth.

Closing her eyes, Julia winced and dropped her chin to her chest, her embroidery lying untouched on her lap. Perhaps even the idea of telling Lord Rushington her name had been foolish. When they had first stepped out together, she had not given a single thought to doing such a thing but, thereafter, upon hearing him speak so honestly to her, hearing his berating of himself and declaring himself a fool, she had found the words coming to her lips regardless. There had been every intention of speaking it to him, having lost herself in a great swell of confusing and conflicting emotions – only for Miss Glover to step forward and interrupt them.

Even now, she found herself wondering what he would have said, had she been honest. Would he have realized the truth? Would he have known who she was, and instantly realized what it was he had done to her? Or would he have simply smiled and thanked her for lifting such a burden from him, without any real awareness of who she was and what he had done to her?

It was perhaps a relief that Miss Glover had interrupted them and reminded Julia that they had not long to return to the carriage. By her doing so, Julia's conversation with Lord Rushington had come to an end. It had been two days since that time and, as yet, she had been unable to stop her thoughts from returning to him over and over again, letting her imagination run furiously over what he might have done or what he could have said, had she revealed the truth.

"We have an invitation!"

Her mother's loud exclamation came flinging itself through the door, only a few seconds before Lady Harbison arrived. Julia set her embroidery aside, looking at her mother with wide eyes.

"An invitation?" These had been few and far between of late, but from the broad smile on her mother's face, Julia's own heart began to quicken. "To what have we been invited?"

"To a Masquerade Ball!" Lady Harbison let out a squeal of excitement as though *she* were the young lady attempting to find a way back into society. "Look, it is to be at the beginning of next week, and we are *all* invited." Grabbing Julia's hand, she squeezed it hard. "Do you understand what this means for you, my dear?"

"I do not, Mama." Frowning, Julia looked at the invitation, and then gently took it from her mother's fingers. "It is a ball, though I am very glad to be invited. Surely this means, however, that I –"

"It is a *Masquerade* Ball," Lady Harbison interrupted, snatching the invitation back again, her eyes roaming greedily across the page. "So no one will be able to identify any other! You will not be a wallflower *this* night, Julia! You will be able to dance and laugh and converse with whomever and whoever you wish… and might have the opportunity to explain what has taken place into one or two ears also."

Julia considered for some moments, not allowing the rising excitement in her chest to overwhelm her.

"I shall be glad to dance, Mama, certainly," she said, slowly, "but I am not certain that speaking to anyone will grant me any favors. Society has forgotten about me and thus, I am thrust into shadow."

"Perhaps they need to simply be reminded that you exist!"

"And in doing so, cause them to recall what occurred that night? To remind them of what they believe about me? That I wound myself through the arms of various gentlemen whilst, at the very same time, supposedly being secretly betrothed?" Julia shook her head, dampening her mother's enthusiasm. "No, I do not think there will be any freedom from my present circumstances, Mama. Though," she continued, letting a small smile curve her lips, "I shall be glad to dance once more. If no one recognizes me, then I shall certainly enjoy the freedom to stand up and dance with whomever chooses to approach me."

"That is something, at least." Her mother sighed and sat down heavily opposite Julia. "I am truly sorry, my dear, for all which has taken place of late. Your father and I have done all that we can but –"

"I am aware of that, Mama." Julia smiled gently, a little regretful of how quickly she had stolen her mother's excitement away. "And I do not blame you, or father, for the situation."

After what had occurred, Lady Harbison had been writing regularly to her husband who had, as promised, returned to his estate long before the incident with Lord Rushington took place. Julia had thought that he might return to London to support her and her mother, but instead, he had remained at the estate. Apparently, matters there were much more pressing.

Lady Harbison smiled, though her eyes were a little glassy.

"It is a difficult situation, certainly." Her sigh came through her words, her eyes closing briefly. "Your father suggested that we return home, and come back to London next Season, in the hope that all will be forgotten." Opening her eyes, she looked directly at Julia. "I confess, I have been considering it."

Julia swallowed hard, a tightness in her chest.

"I do not think that running away would bring any goodness with it, Mama."

"It would not be running away," her mother said, quickly. "It is perhaps only the recognition that this Season has not gone well for you – although none of that is your fault, of course. If we were to come back next Season, then the *ton* might not recall what was said and you would have better opportunities to find a suitable husband." Her eyes searched Julia's face. "I do not want you to suffer, my dear. This has been terribly difficult, I know."

Tears began to swell in Julia's eyes, coming from a heart that bore more pain than she had ever been able to express.

"I understand your concern, Mama, and I am truly appreciative of it," she murmured, doing her utmost not to allow those tears to fall. "And yet, for my part, I believe that returning home and simply praying that all will be well will do no good. The *ton* may forget about what took place, but those that return will still consider me a wallflower, though they might forget the reason I was forced to be so. I do not think that I will ever regain the standing I once had, unless..." Trailing off, she allowed a vision of Lord Rushington to come into her mind. "Unless the gentleman was to admit his mistake to the *ton*," she finished, seeing her mother shake her head.

"Such a thing is not likely, however, is it?" Lady Harbison shook her head and then leaned it back against the couch, slumping in a most unladylike fashion. "That gentleman has stolen so much from you, and given that he has not even *attempted* to make recompense, I am afraid to say that I believe him entirely disinclined towards doing so."

"Perhaps you are right," Julia murmured, reminding herself that, as yet, her mother was entirely unaware of Lord Rushington current thoughts, or of Julia's interest in him. "And you are right about the Masquerade Ball. I *should* be looking forward to the occasion, and I apologize for my lack of enthusiasm." She put a smile on her face and saw the light begin to dance again in her mother's eyes. "I will be able to step forward with every other young lady there, rather than shrink back into the wall. I will be able to hold out my dance card to everyone, rather than have it dangle from my wrist, untouched, for the entirety of the evening." The more she spoke, the more confidence and anticipation began to flood Julia's heart. "I will be able to dance – I will even be able to dance the waltz!"

"Yes, you will be able to," Lady Harbison murmured, pushing herself up so that she sat properly again. "We shall have to make certain that you have an *excellent* mask so that you are remembered by the gentlemen who come to seek you out." Getting up, she walked across the room and gently cupped Julia's chin, looking down into her face. "You deserve contentment and joy in your future, Julia," she murmured, quietly. "I wish this situation had not come upon you, but mayhap there is a way for us to find a suitable gentleman still – one who will ignore the rumors, and see your beauty of face and character and want you by his side."

In an instant, the face of Lord Rushington burned in Julia's mind, and she slid her gaze away from her mother, her face heating.

"Let us hope so, Mama," she murmured quietly, silently wondering why her heart had leaped so fiercely when she had thought of him. Out of all the gentlemen in London, Lord Rushington would not be the one to bring her joy, she was sure of it!

So why did she keep thinking of him?

"GOOD EVENING."

"Good evening," Julia replied, curtseying, and smiling at the gentleman, whose face was barely hidden by the strip of black cutting across his eyes.

Her mother had been right, there *was* something exciting about being fully back within society. No one ignored her, no one walked past her as though she was not there. Her dance card was ready and prepared, her fingers itching to take it from her wrist and hand it to whichever gentleman approached her.

There came a certain freedom in being entirely anonymous. No doubt many of the others within the *ton* felt the same freedom, for rogues, scoundrels, and those with less than stellar reputations were able to simply step in amongst everyone else and hide their true selves – just as she was doing.

Although quite how I am to recognize Lord Rushington, I could not say.

"Might I enquire as to whether you wish to dance this evening, my Lady?"

Julia looked up at the gentleman in question, her smile soft and sweet.

"I fully intend to dance, my Lord."

There was no title she could give him, failing to recognize him even a little. This was certainly *not* Lord Rushington, for his hair was fair and his eyes dark, but all the same, a thrill ran up her spine as she handed him her dance card. He took not one but *two* of her dances, using a simple mark, so as not to give away his identity, and Julia wanted to let out a squeal of sheer delight as she ran her gaze over her card. Surely this evening, she would find herself dancing almost every dance.

"I do hope that neither of those were your waltz, my Lady?"

Another gentleman came close to her, just as the first fellow stepped away. Julia dropped into a curtsey, her heart turning over in her chest as she smiled at the gentleman, her eyes going to what she could see of his features. The dark hair sweeping gently across his forehead, the twinkling of his blue eyes, as well as the fact that his mask barely hid his features left her in no doubt.

This was Lord Rushington.

"Good evening, Lord Rushington."

The gentleman chuckled.

"I have been discovered, it seems."

"It was not particularly difficult to recognize you, but then again, mayhap you were hoping for such a thing?" Tilting her head, she waved her dance card lightly, in a teasing manner, as though it were a fan – only to stop and let her hand fall to her side. Yes, she was to attempt to make him fall in love with her but her feelings, upon seeing and conversing with him, were not those which she wanted to fill her heart. She had been glad to see him, delighted to be in his company again, rather than irritated that he was so full of smiles and obvious happiness after how he had behaved towards her. Where was her indignation? Where was the fiery anger which was to flood her upon remembering what he had done? Why was she so swept away by his smile, her own blossoming forth, unprevented and unblemished?

"Perhaps I was, Miss Smith." When her eyebrow arched, he grinned back at her. "I confess, you were not as easy to single out. In fact, even as I made to approach you, I could not be entirely certain that it *was* you." He put one hand to his heart. "You cannot know how my heart flared when I first caught sight of you. I had not seen you at any other social encounter thus far, but in approaching your company, I permitted myself to hope."

"Then how could you be so sure it *was* I?"

When he chuckled, Julia's cheeks burned and, despite her inner berating of herself, she could not help but smile.

"I could tell when I saw the way that your eyes lit up in response to my question, Miss Smith," he said, his voice a good deal softer now. "I could tell by the delicate curls of your hair by your ears, and by the way your lips curved so gently. You are recognizable to me, it seems, even when you are disguised."

Her heart lurched towards him, and she immediately dropped her eyes to the floor, unable to look into his face, such was the intensity of his gaze. The tenderness of his words was like honey on her tongue, the sweetness warming her very core. When she tried to speak, all that came out was a long, languid breath, followed by a gentle buzzing in her ears in the embarrassed silence that followed for a few moments.

"Should you like to dance with me, Miss Smith?"

She could not find the words to say so, and thus, instead, handed him her dance card without making a single sound. When his head dropped to look at the card, she finally allowed her gaze to rest on him, taking slow, careful breaths so that she might not be overcome.

"I am very glad to see that your waltz is not yet taken, Miss Smith." Lord Rushington's low voice sent a tremble through her limbs. "I can see that the gentleman before me has taken two dances. I hope that you will not think ill of me for doing the same." It was not a question, but rather a statement, and when he handed the dance card back to her, it held his name at both the cotillion and the waltz. "Thereafter, there is to be the unmasking," he murmured, his voice softer still as his fingers brushed across hers, lingering a little too long as she took her dance card again. "Mayhap then, *Miss Smith,* you will provide me with your name – or I shall discover it from another nearby."

A breath of fear caught in Julia's chest. If someone else were to identify her, then she would immediately be recognized as the young lady spurned by society, drab and pitiful in her rejected state. No, she could not permit him to know her name, here!

"Perhaps," she murmured, hoping that her fixed smile was not too apparent. "Now, *do* excuse me, Lord Rushington." Making sure that her smile stretched a little more, she turned away from him directly. "It seems that I am to have a full dance card this evening."

There was no longer as much pleasure in receiving the interest of other gentlemen. Yes, they took her dance card and yes, within the hour, her card was quite full, but all the same, the only thing she could think of, the only thing she could consider, was the unmasking.

What would she do if Lord Rushington demanded to know her name? What if he spoke to someone else, pointing her out and enquiring whether or not they knew her? She could not, she realized, remove her mask in front of him, but to be the only one who did *not,* when the time came, would make her stand out even more.

Whatever was she to do?

CHAPTER THIRTEEN

The waltz was to be the next dance. Benedict smiled to himself, leaning back against the wall, and keeping himself hidden away until the time came. After securing Miss Smith's dances, he had not gone in search of any other, feeling his desire already satisfied.

Prior to this evening, he had not had the opportunity to ask Miss Smith whether or not she would be at the Masquerade and since he did not know her true title, he could not write her a note or the like to enquire. But he had searched for her here, believing that she might attend the Masquerade, knowing her reluctance to be in amongst societal events – although he did not know for what reason.

And now I am to dance the waltz with her.

The thrill such a realization brought had his heart leaping about as if he were already dancing. He had never once held her in his arms in such a way before, though they had walked together many a time, and he had touched her hand upon occasion – but to have her so close during the waltz was a happiness yet to be experienced. Yes, there had been the cotillion, but it did not have the same nearness as the waltz, and it was that closeness which he desired. The unmasking would come thereafter and, given that he would still be with her, he had every intention of finding out her name, one way or the other. Given that she had been close to telling him herself, previously, he could hope that she might reveal it to him of her own accord, when her mask fell away. Or, if she did not, then there were certain to be a good number of gentlemen or ladies of *his* acquaintance who would recognize her. To his mind, it was already a certainty that he would find out the truth, and from that, be able to further their already strong connection.

The next dance was announced, and Benedict stood tall, taking in a long breath before going directly towards Miss Smith. He had been watching her for some time, seeing her step out with various gentlemen and, in doing so, feeling his anticipation growing furiously. Now was the moment when he could take her into his arms, to have her close to him and, with any luck, be offered her name.

Then I can....

He frowned, moving slowly now. Once he discovered her name, what were his intentions? Would he seek to be introduced to her father, so that he might seek permission to court her? To betrothe himself to her? There was so much that he had not yet considered, having been driven by his emotions more than anything else. But... was that not what he had done with Miss Davenport?

"Ah, Lord Rushington. It is to be our waltz, at last."

"It is."

The smile which leaped to his lips had his heart going with it, and when he offered her his arm and she took it with a smile, a heaviness seemed to settle in his heart. No, this was not the same as his feelings had been with Miss Davenport. With Miss Davenport, he had barely given any time to the lady, and had declared himself in love with her before he had even had the opportunity to know anything of her true character. He had been deceived by her – and indeed, he had deceived himself. With Miss Smith, there was no such deceit, he was sure. Yes, she hid her true title from him, but she had admitted, only some days ago, that the reason she did it was simply because she enjoyed teasing him. There was a sense of mystery here, a sweetness about her which could not be mistaken for anything else. Certainly, his heart was affected and yes, his desire for her company was growing ever stronger, but it did not pull at him with the same urgency as that which he had experienced with Miss Davenport. Instead, this had begun as a flicker of interest which now had grown into something big, bright, and full of hope and expectation.

"You are smiling at me, Lord Rushington."

"Is that so peculiar?" The music began and he bowed low before stepping forward. "I think I should always smile when I am with you, Miss Smith."

She stepped into his arms, her chin lifted, her eyes open and fixed to his. He put one hand to her waist, the other clasping her hand, and the waltz began.

Benedict had thought that he might offer some conversation, for the waltz did allow a few words here and there. Now, however, as he looked down into her eyes, Benedict felt robbed of speech. All of his expectations had been building, to the point that they now exploded like the fireworks he had watched with her at Vauxhall Gardens. This was wonderful. To have her so near him, her hand held tightly in his, the music encouraging them ever closer as they whirled gently around, was pouring affection into his heart. It could not be denied, not when his heart was leaping around with such happiness, not when the smile on his face simply would not dim, even a little. Miss Smith was someone he could not escape from, whom he could not step back from, or leave behind. He wanted to dance every waltz with her, wanted to be even closer to her if he could. It was not as if he were about to leap into betrothal again, but what he felt was so very strong, he had no other choice but to respond to it.

I must seek to court her.

The words came to his lips, but he could not speak them. All that followed was a ragged breath. Miss Smith continued to look up at him, though her eyes were a little shadowed, a slight frown across her face. Was it that she did not understand why they were no longer speaking? Why he had danced in silence thus far? Or was it that she could see the play of emotions across his face and was wondering what each one meant?

The music began to slow, and Benedict wanted to shout out in protest, his hands tightening a little on Miss Smith. Was it not that they had only just begun to dance? To him, it was as if the music had been played for only a few seconds, and had not given him enough time to dance with Miss Smith.

"You frown now, instead of smiling." Miss Smith stepped back from him, the heat between them fading rapidly, and her voice somewhat quiet. "I do hope that I have not upset you."

"No, not in the least." Benedict bowed and then turned to her, his arm out for her to take. "I will admit to frowning, but it came from a silent disagreement with the orchestra."

Miss Smith laughed at this, her eyes sparking with humor.

"Is that so? And what, pray tell, was your disagreement?"

"I think that they played for far too short a time," he declared, firmly. "It was not as long as it ought to have been. Either that or I lost all sense of time during our waltz together... though that may very well have been the reason for such a feeling, I admit it." When his gaze slid towards her, there was a pink in what he could see of her cheeks, but she was not looking at him any longer. Benedict smiled to himself but said nothing further, realizing quickly that he had no thought of where he ought to take the lady. Did she have a companion or her mother here with her?

"Miss Smith, I realize that –"

"And now comes the unmasking!" Lord Masterton, their host for the evening, cried out in his usual loud voice, and soon, a quiet hush began to fall across the room. "The orchestra will play, and when it comes to a stop, we shall all remove our masks and delight in the companions we discover!"

Before Benedict could react, Miss Smith was gone. He turned hastily, seeing her scurrying away with rapid steps. A little surprised, he hurried after her as she slipped into the shadows at the very edge of the room.

"Miss Smith?" Putting out one hand, he caught her arm, pulling her back lightly before dropping his hand again. "Are you quite well?"

"Very well, thank you."

Benedict frowned, noting how she looked from left to right, and taking in the red in what he could see of her cheeks.

"I should take you back to whomever you arrived with. I did not know –"

"I am quite well, I thank you. It is only that, with the unmasking, I –"

"You cannot be afraid to show your face to me," Benedict interrupted, moving a little closer. "We are already known to each other. Why would you have any fear over that?" Reaching out, he snared her hand again, but was ready to release it if she made even the slightest protest. "If there is something the matter, Miss Smith, then allow me to be of aid to you in some way. You appear a little distressed, and I want to make certain that you are well. I cannot permit you to hurry away from me, not when you have no one else with you. It would not be right."

Miss Smith said nothing for a few moments, the only sound her brief sigh. Her fingers tightened around his and she lifted her chin, looking straight up at him as the orchestra continued to play. There was laughter and conversation all around them, an excited hubbub of noise, but all Benedict could hear was Miss Smith.

"Do you truly care for me in that regard, Lord Rushington?"

"Of course I do." A frown flickered across his forehead. "I would not force you to remain, my dear lady, but I am a little worried, I confess it. I do not understand why you would run from me, and given that I can see no-one nearby looking for you, my concern grows even more. Surely there must be someone who –"

"And begin!"

The cry of Lord Masterton had a huge cheer erupting from the center of the ballroom. Everyone began to remove their masks and Benedict, not wishing to be the only one left with his mask still tied to his face, removed it at once.

Miss Smith did not.

Frowning, Benedict looked at her, perplexed as to her stillness. Her fingers did not lift to her head, the mask did not fall from her face.

"Miss Smith?" His heart was pounding wildly, now

filled with an uncertainty that bubbled over into his voice. "What is the matter?" His fingers pressed hers. "If I can be of aid to you, if I can help you in any way, then I beg of you only to ask me. I am your willing servant, I assure you."

Miss Smith dropped her head forward, hiding her face from him. Her other hand lifted to the back of her head and, after only a few seconds, the mask on her face fell away, caught by one nimble hand. Then she lifted her head and looked directly at him, her eyes suddenly piercing his. There was a sheen in her eyes which he could not understand, and her cheeks were still a soft pink.

"Oh, Lord Rushington." Closing her eyes, Miss Smith took in a shaky breath, then let it out again as she looked at him. "Whatever am I to do?"

There was a hint of agony in her words and Benedict blinked, his chest tightening with confusion as Miss Smith stepped forward and boldly put her free hand to his shoulder. He glanced at it, opening his mouth to say something only for her to push herself up on tiptoe, look deeply into his eyes for a long moment, and then press her mouth to his.

CHAPTER FOURTEEN

I do not think I have ever done anything so foolish.
Julia closed her eyes tightly only for a single tear to drop onto her cheek. It had not been her thought to kiss Lord Rushington but, regardless of whether or not she had meant to, she *had* done it, and now could not take back the moment she had done so.

Another tear fell to her cheek.

Perhaps I do not wish to, either.

"Miss Glover, my Lady."

Julia made to get up hastily, only for Miss Glover's exclamation to ring around the room, having spotted the fact that Julia was in some sort of distress.

"My dear friend, whatever is the matter?" Miss Glover was beside her at once, taking her hand and squeezing it gently. "Is it the Masquerade Ball? I have come to speak with you about it, this very minute! I was so eager to know whether you had enjoyed yourself for, from what I observed, you had every dance taken."

"And now I am to go back to being a wallflower," Julia sniffed, knowing that this was not the true reason for her tears. "It was a wonderful evening, but it makes me all too aware of my present situation. My father thinks that I ought to return to the estate, then come back to London next Season and now, after what I have done, I begin to wonder if it would not be for the best."

Miss Glover blinked, a line between her brows.

"What you have done?" she repeated, as Julia's face burned with the realization of what she had said. "Whatever do you mean?"

Swallowing the lump in her throat, Julia sniffed again, and then took the handkerchief offered her with a word of thanks.

"You told me to be careful, Mary, and I think I ought to have listened a little more."

Miss Glover's eyes flared in sudden understanding.

"Oh. This is to do with Lord Rushington?"

"Yes, of course it is."

"I do not think that you need to return to your father's estate because of him," Miss Glover stated, plainly. "Perhaps you ought to talk to Lord Rushington? Explain everything, from the very beginning. I am sure that he will be willing to make some sort of pronouncement, which will encourage the *ton* to return you to your former place. It is clear that he cares about you, and I am quite certain that he will be more than willing to help you. I am aware you wished to punish him but –"

"I kissed him."

Her words seemed to whisper into every corner, every nook of the room, becoming so loud and repeated so many times that Julia cringed and then hid her face from her friend by burying it in her hands. Miss Glover's expression, before Julia had turned away, had been one of utter shock. Her eyes were fixed wide, her mouth in a perfect circle, and her face a little pale. No doubt it was the last thing she had expected to hear from Julia.

"Goodness."

The hoarseness of Miss Glover's voice made Julia want to weep with mortification.

"I did not mean to do it." Her hands fell back to her lap as she attempted to explain herself. "It was not something I had given any thought to, truly! I was afraid."

"Afraid?" Miss Glover repeated, her voice now a little stronger. "What were you afraid of?"

Julia sniffed and dabbed her eyes again with the handkerchief.

"I was afraid of what I felt during our waltz together. I was terrified of taking my mask from my face and revealing myself – not only to him, but to everyone else present."

Miss Glover nodded slowly, her shoulders dropping a fraction.

"I understand. You were afraid that, if he should point you out to an acquaintance or a friend, they would identify you as the young lady he had spurned, and that, no doubt, would cause all manner of confusion."

Julia nodded, a pain beginning to spread up across her chest.

"And because he would turn from me." Those words came out in a whisper, and she looked away again. "These last few weeks, I have fought to keep my feelings contained. I have reminded myself of what he has done, and the position I am now in because of him. I have told myself that he is heedless to his folly, and uncaring about what has become of that young lady. I have told myself these things many a time and yet, despite that, the anger I have tried to cling onto insists on fading away, bit by bit."

"Leaving you feeling something more?"

Miserable, Julia could give no other answer than a nod.

"And you feared that, if he realized the truth, and suffered the confusion which would follow, you would lose his companionship forever?"

Again, Julia nodded.

"It is so very troubling. I wanted to break his heart, to triumph over him, to take away something in the same way as he took something from me. Instead, I now find my heart to be so desperate for him that it does not *want* to bring him any harm! Instead, it seeks to find a way to bring us closer – but how I can I even *think* of that when I know what I have done?"

"You have done nothing as yet," Miss Glover consoled. "You had intentions to be vengeful, yes but you did not act upon them."

Julia shook her head, her handkerchief squashed up in between her fingers.

"I would not be able to explain myself away without telling him everything. He will know that I recognized him, that I have always known who he was, and what he did. There will be no explanation for him as to my willingness to grow closer, save for the truth which I have held onto so tightly."

"And do you think that you could share that with him?"

Miss Glover's quiet voice sent her question ricocheting around Julia's mind. Could she do that? *Would* she? It would mean explaining all to Lord Rushington, from the very beginning, informing him of her intentions and what had happened thereafter.

A thread of worry began to push itself through her veins.

"I fear for what would happen if I did," she answered, truthfully. "Mary, he would have every right to step away from me, to push me back as far as he could! I would be another Miss Davenport to him, another who did not tell him the truth and who treated him as though all was well when it was not!"

Miss Glover held her gaze steadily.

"Then what is the alternative, Julia? Will you pretend to be 'Miss Smith' forever? You know such a thing cannot happen."

"No, it cannot, which is why you now find me in this state of distress." Julia sniffed as fresh tears came to her eyes and she allowed them to fall, managing to catch most of them with her handkerchief. "I do not know what to do. The very thing which I promised myself I would not permit to occur has happened. I *care* for Lord Rushington, he is within my heart, and yet our connection was born out of deliberate, dark intentions on my part. The only thing I can do, I think, is to step away from him."

A slight frown rippled across Miss Glover's features.

"You mean, you want to step away from him entirely?"

"Yes." The thought of it tore gouges in her heart, but her chin lifted, a resolve beginning to fill her. "That would be for the best. I have no real desire to do so, for my heart yearns to be in his company again, but if I cannot tell him the truth, and I cannot permit myself to grow close to him, then perhaps I ought to make certain that I cannot so much as see him again."

Miss Glover frowned.

"What does that mean?"

"It means that I shall return to my father's estate, as he has suggested." The words brought a heaviness to her soul, and she lowered her head and let her shoulders round. "It is the only thing I can think to do."

There were a few moments of silence, followed only by

a huff of breath from Miss Glover and a gentle clicking of her tongue.

"I can understand why you might want to run away, but it does not solve your problem, Julia."

Julia looked back into Miss Glover's face.

"What do you mean? Of course it does. If he stays here and I go back to my father's estate, then –"

"Then he will be here *next* Season," her friend interrupted, quietly. "And no doubt, he will find you out and demand to know what you meant by running away as you did. Or he will discover the truth during this Season, and you may find yourself with either an unexpected visitor or letters which you must reply to. Removing yourself from London will not bring you any sort of satisfaction or relief."

"I do not think that he would do such a thing as come to my father's estate to find out the truth. I do not believe that I mean so much to him."

Julia tried to put confidence into her voice, but Miss Glover only lifted one eyebrow and held her gaze fixedly, to the point that Julia was forced to drop her eyes and look away.

"You must know that he cares for you too." The softness of Miss Glover's voice and the kindness in the squeeze of her hand pulled a sob from Julia's chest. "I do not say such things to upset you, only to state that I believe that Lord Rushington truly does care for you. He would not be so eager to walk with you, to talk so openly with you about all that has taken place this Season, if he did not have an affection for you. Trust me, my dear friend, you may try to escape from Lord Rushington, but I do not think you will be able to. Even if you return to your father's estate, you will take him with you, in your heart, and I am sure, thereafter, will become all the more sorrowful." Shifting in her seat, she leaned closer to Julia, bending her head a little. "Would it not be wise to try to resolve the matter here? Even if you are left with a broken heart, you would be assured that he knows all and understands everything... including the state of your own heart."

Julia closed her eyes and tried to find the right words to offer up as an answer, but none were given to her. Instead, she could only lift her shoulders and let them fall, her emotions bound up so tightly that she feared a single word would break them apart, shattering her completely.

—

"My dear Lord Rushington," Julia murmured aloud, her quill scratching across the paper, then became silent as the words continued to flow onto the page.

'It has been almost a sennight since the Masquerade Ball – a fact I am sure you are all too aware of. As you may have suspected, I have remained away from society for a time. However, I do wish to see you again.'

Julia closed her eyes tightly, aware of the tremble that ran across her as she penned those words. Yes, she had come to a resolution when it came to Lord Rushington – she *did* want to see him, and did want to find a way to tell him the truth, but all the same, there was a great fear in that.

I must do this.

Miss Glover had spoken a great deal of sense, and whilst Julia had rebelled against the idea of being honest with him, she had soon realized that escaping back to her father's estate would bring her more difficulty, just as Miss Glover had pointed out. Therefore, she had no other choice but to be as courageous as she could... even if it meant pushing Lord Rushington away from her forever.

Putting her quill back into the inkpot, she steeled herself and continued to write.

'I hoped we might take another short walk through the park – perhaps Hyde Park, this time? I shall be there tomorrow afternoon, at three o'clock sharp. I do hope that you will be able to join me. There is a good deal I wish to discuss with you.'

"My dear?" Julia turned her head sharply, just as her mother walked into the room. There was a flickering concern in her eyes, and in the way that she tilted her head just a little, her hands clasped together in front of her. "You have been absent for most of the afternoon," Lady Harbison continued, making her way slowly across towards Julia, but coming to a stop a short distance away, so she could not read her letter. "In fact, I should say that you have been absent from my company ever since the Masquerade Ball. You have been hiding yourself away and, I confess, I am concerned."

"You need not be, Mama." With a breath, Julia sanded the letter, relieved that she had something to do, instead of looking back at her mother. "All will be well, I assure you."

One glance towards Lady Harbison told Julia that she was not about to be so easily believed.

"You almost ran from the Masquerade," she continued, as Julia folded up the letter and began to prepare the wax. "I understand that it may have come from a fear of being recognized and, thereafter, being rejected and pushed away by the other guests, but might I ask if that was the only reason?"

Julia swallowed hard.

"What other reason would there be, Mama?"

Lady Harbison let out a breath and shook her head, her lips gently pursed. Julia's heart ached, but she did not permit herself to say anything further. Whilst she appreciated her mother's concern, to tell her the truth would not be wise. No doubt it would only upset her mother, and Julia did not want to add to her mother's already heavy burden.

"If there was something more, I should like you to know that I would be glad to have you share it with me." There was a hint of sadness whispering about her mother's words, and Julia swallowed at the tears beginning to lodge in her throat. "I do not like to see you suffer, Julia. You have endured so much already."

Julia managed a small smile, but then looked away, returning her attention to the letter.

"All will be well, Mama. It has been something of a trying Season, I confess, but I will be contented again very soon."

Taking the wax, she dripped some of it carefully down onto the fold of the letter, closing it up.

"You are not going to press our seal into it?"

Julia pressed her lips together, looking at her mother.

"No, not with this letter."

"What is contained within it?"

Lady Harbison's eyes flared with alarm, and she came closer, only for Julia to put one hand on her mother's arm.

"It is to Lord Rushington," she said, honestly.

"Rushington?"

Closing her eyes briefly, Julia's stomach lurched. Thus far, she had kept all of her dealings with Lord Rushington to herself and had never once told her mother about him or that she had identified him as the responsible gentleman. After all, her mother had warned her of the man, and then commanded her to forget his very existence – so she'd had good reason not to let her mother know... Her mother's face had darkened into what looked like disbelief.

"Lord Rushington is the gentleman who caused my descent within society." She spoke quickly, hearing her mother's swift intake of breath. "He was the one who mistook me for someone else. Thus far, however, he has not recognized me, and therefore, I now feel eager to speak with him about what took place."

Lady Harbison put one hand to her forehead.

"Good gracious, Julia. How long have you known this? Why did you not tell me?"

Choosing to only answer the latter question, Julia rose to her feet, letter in hand.

"Because there was already enough of a struggle, Mama. When I first met Lord Rushington, there was not a single flicker of recognition upon his face – which mayhap ought not to surprise me, given his confusion that evening. However, after some time considering, I have now decided that I must tell him the truth, in the hope that, in some way, he will be able to restore me to the standing I had before." She smiled softly and took her mother's hand. "I must meet with him. I must *speak* with him, and tell him all. And that is what this letter is for."

Lady Harbison's eyes glistened with tears, but she nodded, a watery smile on her lips.

"You have more strength in you than I credited you with," came the quiet reply. "I do hope that Lord Rushington will do as you hope, his past reputation notwithstanding."

Julia swallowed thickly, her smile a little slow in returning to her lips.

"I hope that he will listen." Letting go of her mother's hand, she went to ring the bell, murmuring quietly to herself. "And that he will not push me further away than I have ever been from him before."

CHAPTER FIFTEEN

"You may think that you escaped the notice of all and sundry, but I can assure you that you need not hide it from me." Lord Burnley slapped Benedict hard on the shoulder, causing him to fall forward and then catch himself in surprise. "I do not know why you have not spoken to me of it as yet - it has been a sennight at least!"

Benedict rolled his eyes at Lord Burnley's broad grin.

"If you would like to inform me of what you are speaking about, I would be grateful."

Lord Burnley's grin only grew, his eyes sparking with interest, and a little mirth, but Benedict's spirits did not lift. They had been sinking all the lower with every day that passed, with every day that Miss Smith did not reach out to him. He had not seen her, had not received a note from her, and even though he had met Miss Glover at a soiree only two days previous, she had not had a single word for him. To have Lord Burnley now grinning madly at him was only adding to his irritation.

"You will not speak of it?" Lord Burnley gave up

waiting for Benedict to say something of his own volition, and instead laughed and shrugged his shoulders. "Then permit me to do so. I was there the night of the Masquerade Ball. I took my mask from my face, bowed over the hand of the *exceptionally* beautiful young lady I had been dancing with... only for my eye to catch sight of you and another young lady in a certain embrace." His eyebrows lifted high. "I must confess to being rather surprised that you would be as bold as all that."

Benedict scowled and shook his head.

"You will be all the more surprised when I tell you that I was not the one who initiated such an embrace." As he had expected, Lord Burnley's eyebrows immediately lifted dramatically, and the grin began to shrink away. "And no, I have not seen the lady in question since," Benedict continued before Lord Burnley could say anything. "I should be glad if you would not speak of this to anyone else either."

Lord Burnley put one hand to his heart, his grin swiftly returning, although he attempted to look injured also.

"How could you even *consider* that I would do such a thing?" With a chuckle, his hand fell back to his side. "No, I have not spoken to anyone about what I witnessed, although I must say that you are fortunate indeed that no one else has said a word about it! Yes, you were in shadow, but you were not entirely hidden."

"Again, it was not my doing." Benedict shuffled his feet, the shock of what had taken place suddenly washing over him again. "It was unexpected."

"But not disagreeable?"

With a long breath, Benedict dropped his shoulders and looked his friend straight in the eye.

"No, not displeasing," he confessed, quietly. "Not in the

least. What troubles me now is that I have not spoken to the lady."

Lord Burnley's smile fell completely.

"I can see that does concern you. It was not some foolish bet, then? Not a moment of madness whereupon you acted on a feeling of desire?"

"No." Benedict shook his head. "Nothing like that. This young lady means a great deal to me, even though I do not even know her real name."

Blinking, Lord Burnley put out his hands.

"How can such a thing be? If this young lady is the same one you were trying so *very* hard to ignore when we met in the park some time ago, then surely you must know her name by now?"

Benedict's smile was rueful.

"You recognized that, then?" Sighing, he rubbed one hand over his eyes. "Perhaps I ought not to have pretended."

"What was your reason for doing so?"

Closing his eyes again, Benedict pinched the bridge of his nose, aware that the explanation was long and convoluted.

"The connection between myself and Miss Smith – for that is what I know her as – has been somewhat mysterious. When we were out in the park together, when I made what I thought was the distinct impression that I was not acquainted with Miss Smith, it was because I wished to preserve that connection. It was for myself only, I believed and thus, I did not want to introduce her. Perhaps I ought to have been truthful, but I was not. I hope I did not injure you."

"You did not." Lord Burnley shrugged, his smile still present. "Though I admit to being a little confused as to why you do not yet know her real name, especially after you kissed her." Seeing Benedict's frown, he laughed and rolled his eyes. "After she kissed *you*, of course."

Benedict's heart twisted as he continued with his explanation.

"How can I write to her if I do not know where she lives? I do not know the name of her father or any other of her acquaintances, save for Miss Glover, who has said nothing to me, I might add. I can do nothing but wait for her."

"Or you might ask about her?" Lord Burnley's suggestion burned Benedict's ears. "Yes, it would mean making sure that there were others within the *ton* who knew of your connection to the lady but, all the same, it would be a way to find her out, would it not?"

Benedict nodded but did not instantly agree.

"There is something about Miss Smith that makes her stay back from society," he said, slowly, seeing his friend frown. "I do not fully understand it, but I find a reluctance within myself to go about asking questions for fear that she would be displeased with me doing so."

"Then you will wait," came the quick response. "You will wait, and you will wait, and you will wait."

"I do not know how long it will be for," Benedict stated, a trifle irritated by Lord Burnley's obvious statement. "She may appear at any time. She may –"

Lord Burnley cut the air between them with a flat hand.

"Rushington. I can see that there is something about this lady that intrigues you – more than that, in fact, it seems to tie you to her. You consider her feelings more than your own. Your concern is for *her* rather than yourself. Your heart is clearly involved. If you love her, then ought you not do all that you can to profess that to her?"

Benedict opened his mouth to state that no, he could

not be in love with her, only to snap it closed again, his brow furrowing hard. Could it be true? Could he be in love with the lady?

"I have an affection for her, certainly." The words came out slowly, one after the other. "But love is not something I can be sure of. I believed myself in love with Miss Davenport. While I am aware that those feelings did not have any real basis, and that I was foolish in allowing myself to feel so much, so quickly, I do not want to rush into admitting any great depth of emotion."

Lord Burnley did not laugh, however, as Benedict had expected. Instead, he merely looked back at Benedict without saying a word, the seconds ticking by into stillness. A little awkward, Benedict shuffled his feet again and looked down at the ground, wondering if he ought to say more, just as Lord Burnley heaved a great and obvious sigh.

"I can offer you nothing in the way of further advice, for the experience of a deepening affection and love for a young lady is not something I have known," he admitted, though his tone sounded a little sorrowful as though he regretted never once having been in love. "Only that I should think it best if you tell the lady how you feel... though I can understand that it may prove difficult if you cannot even *find* the lady!"

"Indeed."

"Then ask." Looking around, Lord Burnley gestured to the room filled with people. Lord Fletherworth's soiree was certainly busy enough. "Perhaps if you made some discreet enquiries, you would be able to ascertain a few potential names for the lady."

Benedict pressed his lips tight together, filled his lungs with air, and then released the breath quickly. If he was nearing the state of being in love with Miss Smith, then he *had* to do something about the matter. If she had not come to him during this last sennight, then he *had* to do something to discover her. He would go mad otherwise.

"Very well."

Lord Burnley's eyes flared.

"Truly? Come then. I know precisely who we ought to ask."

∼

Benedict threw his friend a sharp look.

"You wish to approach Lady Duncastle?"

"Why ever not?"

"She is the biggest gossip in all of London, that is why not."

"Which is precisely *why* we ought to speak with her," Lord Burnley explained, sounding a little impatient. "She will know who this young lady is, I am certain of it."

Benedict tugged his mouth to one side.

"Mayhap, but recall that Miss Smith is not particularly keen on society. I do not want to do anything which might embarrass her."

"Which I understand." Throwing out one hand towards Lady Duncastle, Lord Burnley lifted an eyebrow. "Well?"

Resisting the urge to sigh, Benedict nodded and stepped forward, his hands curling into tight fists, not because he was angry, but more as a result of the nervousness which flooded him. He did not want to do anything which might drive Miss Smith away from him. He would have to be careful.

After some minutes of conversation – a conversation which Benedict had no interest in, given that it concerned the current whereabouts of Lord Kingshill and Lady

Woodridge – Benedict caught the sharp look that Lord Burnley sent him, which was followed by his attempt to push the topic of Miss Smith into conversation.

"Did you know that Lord Rushington has made a new acquaintance of late?" Before Benedict could even consider saying anything, Lord Burnley continued, grinning broadly when Benedict glared at him. "But he will not tell me much about her!"

"Is that so?" Lady Duncastle chuckled, her eyes glinting with obvious interest. "And will you not speak of her because you wish to keep her presence a secret? Or because you fear that Lord Burnley might steal her from you?"

Her laughter had Lord Burnley chuckling, although Benedict remained stoic.

"I think that it is perhaps both, my Lady," Lord Burnley said, making Lady Duncastle break into peals of laughter. "Although I confess, I do understand why Lord Rushington is cautious."

Immediately, Lady Duncastle sobered.

"Yes, of course. After what took place with that *disgraceful* young lady, I am not in the least bit surprised."

"Thank you." Benedict shot another fiery look to Lord Burnley, begging him silently to remain quiet, but his friend only shrugged. "This is a new acquaintance, as Lord Burnley has said, and I want to make certain that all is well before I think of telling Lord Burnley anything of my opinions on the lady. I shall not be as foolish as I was previously!"

"Indeed." Lady Duncastle put a hand to his arm, her eyes glinting with a gentle sympathy which surprised him. "It must be very difficult indeed to have your betrothal ended so suddenly. I confess to you now that I did not hear exactly what happened, but…"

Trailing off, she kept her eyes fixed on his and Benedict frowned, wondering if this was her way of silently asking him to tell her everything. A quick yet surreptitious nod from Lord Burnley confirmed to him that this was a way to make certain that his questions about Miss Smith were answered and thus, he began.

"I believed myself to have a deep affection for the lady," he began, the words coming out quickly, but without pain. "I proposed and she accepted. Only a few days thereafter, I caught her in the arms of another gentleman... and then quite lost my wits." Cringing, he looked away from Lady Duncastle's sparkling eyes. "It was my own foolishness, however. I have learned from that now."

Lady Duncastle clicked her tongue.

"Do not berate yourself too harshly, Lord Rushington."

"You are very kind."

"And I do hope that you feel no guilt in speaking as you did!" Lady Duncastle's hand was back on his arm, squeezing it gently. "It was right for the *ton* to know of her behavior! Any other gentleman who might consider her would no longer do so and that is a relief in itself!"

Benedict blinked, then allowed a line to form between his brows as he looked first at Lady Duncastle and then at Lord Burnley. A stone dropped into the pit of his stomach.

"You are speaking of the evening when I behaved very poorly indeed, are you not?"

"Yes. You look confused, Lord Rushington."

"I am not confused," Benedict answered, speaking slowly as a sheen of sweat broke out across his forehead. "Forgive me for my silence. It is only that I thought..."

His eyes squeezed closed. A fire was beginning to grow within Benedict's chest. His heart was beating furiously, his stomach twisting this way and that as guilt swam through him.

I thought that evening had been forgotten. I did not think that the young lady whom I confused for Miss Davenport would be cruelly treated by society. Was I mistaken in that belief?

"You will have witnessed all, Lady Duncastle," he continued, as the lady nodded, her eyes on his face. "You saw how I reacted towards that young lady on the evening of the Ball."

"Yes." She threw up her hands. "But why do you appear so concerned? It was just as she deserved, and I should not permit yourself to feel any guilt over it!"

"Oh, but I do," Benedict said, quickly, taking a small step closer to her, his heart pounding. "The lady I spoke to so angrily, that is who you believe I was betrothed to?"

"But of course." Lady Duncastle's frown returned, and her eyes were sharp on his face. "Everyone did. I saw her as she took her leave with her mother and, of course, I could not allow such a thing to escape without notice!"

Benedict closed his eyes.

"You took what had happened and told others?"

He knew the answer to his question before he asked it, and, seeing the lady nod, he felt a weight slamming down upon his shoulders.

"Yes, I certainly did. A young lady had accepted your proposal and thereafter, had chosen to throw your consideration of her away! She did not even have the courtesy to explain herself to you but, from what I understood, placed herself into the arms of another gentleman without so much as a thought of you. I spoke of it to those I trusted, so that the other gentlemen of London would know to stay far from her."

A small, crooked smile pulled at Lady Duncastle's lips, as if she were pleased by what she had done rather than feeling any embarrassment over being so willing to spread gossip. "I am glad to see that the young lady has been forced to face the consequences of her actions – as regards society, at least."

Benedict wanted to cry out aloud, the anguish of what he had done tearing him asunder. He had gone to his estate to see his sister wed without even a single thought of what would happen next. At the time, he had believed it to be Miss Davenport he had spoken with, but then, once he had discovered that it was not her whom he had thrown his harsh words at, he had done nothing to resolve the matter. Two brief conversations with Lord Burnley had been enough to assuage his guilt... but he now realized just how much he had failed this young lady.

"Do you mean to say that she left London?"

There was barely any strength to his voice, causing Lady Duncastle to eye him suspiciously.

"No," she answered, speaking slowly now. "No, she remained in London – though quite why she should wish to do so, I cannot understand! What I mean is that all of London society pulled back from her. I have seen her on occasion, but she is nothing more than a wallflower now. No gentleman approaches her, no lady seeks her out in the hope of friendship. I think it would be best if she returned home, but mayhap she still hopes that there is something which can be salvaged from the disastrous state she has left herself in."

It was as if he were being pushed into the floor, such was the heaviness of his guilt and shame. Running one hand down his face, Benedict could not help but emit a groan, though it was only Lady Duncastle who appeared surprised. Lord Burnley was also a little pale, one hand rubbing his chin, his eyes darting from place to place.

Closing his eyes tightly, Benedict steadied himself.

"Might I ask, Lady Duncastle, what the name of this unfortunate lady is?" When his eyes snapped open, Lady Duncastle's mouth had fallen open, her eyes wide. "I understand that you think I should already be aware of her name, but I assure you, I am not. There has been a mistake – a dreadful mistake. It was to Miss *Davenport* I was betrothed, but it was not she who I spoke to that evening. I was, regrettably, in my cups, and befuddled enough to mistake her."

It took Lady Duncastle a few moments to understand what he meant. Her eyes searched his face, only for her hand to fly to her mouth in obvious horror at the part she had unwittingly played.

"Her name, Lady Duncastle, *please.*"

"Miss Davenport is now married," Lady Duncastle whispered, her hand dropping back to her side. "You thought that you spoke to Miss Davenport?"

"I did. The name?"

A desperation hurried his heart into a frantic beat as Lady Duncastle swayed just a little, clearly no longer as poised as before. Benedict wanted to grab her arms and shake her, to force the words from her if he could, but he held himself still until the lady let out a slow breath.

"That unfortunate young lady is Miss Morningside." Her whisper ran towards Benedict and tied itself like a noose around his neck. "Her father is Viscount Harbison."

"Harbison." Benedict blinked furiously, trying desperately to recall if he had ever heard that name before, but finding his mind empty. "Thank you, Lady Duncastle – and please, do excuse me. There is much for me to think on."

CHAPTER SIXTEEN

"You had a visitor during your absence, my Lady."

Julia turned in surprise, her lady's maid offering her a small smile.

"Did I?"

"It was a gentleman," the maid continued, coming to help Julia prepare for her afternoon walk. "I do not know a great deal, but he appeared to be in some distress. I heard his exclamations from the hallway."

"Oh?" A frown made its way across Julia's forehead. "How very strange."

The maid nodded and began to adjust Julia's hair, fixing it just a little here and there as she sat at her dressing table.

"He asked for your father at first, and then for Lady Harbison thereafter, but stated, quite clearly, he simply *had* to speak with you."

Julia's frown grew ever deeper.

"That is unusual. Did he leave a card?"

"I think he did, my Lady. Your mother will have it, of course."

"Of course." Julia took a breath and set her shoulders,

looking at her reflection in the mirror. "I shall speak to her about it later. I must be ready for the arrival of Miss Glover's carriage. I do not want to be tardy."

The maid nodded, then placed Julia's bonnet on her head, leaving her to tie the ribbons.

"And are there any plans for this evening, my Lady? Should I lay out a gown?"

Julia shook her head and ignored the twist in her stomach. There was not to be a Ball, soiree, or dinner tonight, as had become expected. Nowadays, she was not the recipient of many invitations. It was strange to realize that she had not found the situation unbearable, not since Lord Rushington had become more important to her.

At the thought of him, a tremor ran through Julia's frame, and she quickly rose to her feet, wanting to hide it from the maid. There was so much she had to say, so much she wanted to express to him, but the fear of what he might do once he heard the truth from her lips gave her the greatest consternation.

There came a tap at the door, and the footman called to her.

"My Lady, Miss Glover's carriage has arrived."

Julia turned to her maid hastily.

"No, there is to be no gown or the like. I shall return shortly."

The maid nodded and Julia hurried away, only for her mother's voice to come chasing after her.

"Julia?"

"I am to go for a carriage ride with Miss Glover, Mama," Julia called back, her steps quick on the staircase. "Her carriage has arrived, and I must not be late." Glancing over her shoulder to where her mother stood at the top of the staircase, Julia paused for a brief moment, seeing the way her mother's lips had pursed.

"Mama?"

Lady Harbison started slightly, only to nod, smile, and wave her daughter away.

"It will keep," she said, quietly. "Go."

Julia's feet remained where they were.

"Is it about the gentleman caller?" she asked, only for her mother's brows to lower over her eyes.

Seeing that there would be no answer, Julia merely smiled and continued to make her way to the carriage.

"You do not look as flustered as I feared." Miss Glover's warm smile helped Julia's breathing to settle as she sat down opposite her friend. "I am sure that all will go well."

"I am only grateful to you for your willingness, and your aid in this matter," Julia answered, pressing one hand lightly to her forehead, before setting both hands in her lap again. "I do not think that my mother would permit me to depart the house without your company and, given the situation, I do not think that I could explain all to her."

"But of course." Reaching across, Miss Glover squeezed Julia's hand. "All will be well, I am sure."

"I must hope so." Julia closed her eyes and did not allow the threads of tension to wrap themselves together into a stronger twist. "I fear that he may turn around and walk away from me!"

"And if he does, then at least you will be comforted that you have told him the truth," Miss Glover said softly. "Now, do not let your thoughts dwell on what might happen. Let us talk of something else so that you do not become either overly pale or hot and flustered!"

Julia smiled, but it disappeared almost instantly.

"I do not think that I can take my thoughts to anything else."

"Then I shall talk for us both," Miss Glover declared, before launching into such a prolonged speech that Julia had no hope of doing anything other than listen as the carriage rolled its way towards Hyde Park, and the waiting Lord Rushington.

∽

"Lord Rushington?" Julia's heart was beating so furiously, it sent a wave of nausea rolling up through her. She curtsied and pulled her eyes from him as he turned around, having been standing with his hands clasped behind his back. "Forgive me for being a little tardy."

"You shall have to forgive me also, Miss Smith."

Lord Rushington inclined his head, but when he lifted it again, his eyes were filled with a darkness she had never seen before. A shudder ran through her. Did he already know the truth? Had he somehow discovered it all?

"And why must she forgive you?" Miss Glover's cheerful voice broke through the tension as she came to stand directly beside Julia, her hand on her arm. "Whatever is it that you have done?"

Lord Rushington attempted to smile, but it fell away.

"It is not what I have done but what I must do. I fear that I must step away almost as soon as I am arrived. I received your letter, but while I understand that there is an importance for you to speak with me, there is something which holds even greater sway over me, and which I cannot be dissuaded from. I have already tried to set it to rights but..." Closing his eyes, he let out a sigh and then, opening them again, looked straight at Julia. "Had I known your name or the house you reside in, I would have come to speak with you or written a note to inform you of this. Instead, I had no choice but to linger here."

"I understand." The fear that had wrapped around her heart began to loosen. "Whatever is the matter, Lord Rushington? I do hope that it is not your sister?"

He let out a bark of harsh laughter which made her jump.

"No, it is not, Miss Smith, though I thank you for your concern. It is a matter which has only just come to my attention, but which is entirely because of my own foolishness, my own senseless arrogance and inconsideration. In short, Miss Smith, Miss Glover, I have injured someone without intentionality – but have done nothing to lessen such an injury in the time thereafter."

Julia's fingers wrapped around Miss Glover's hand, her heart now coming to a stop before slamming hard against her chest again. Her every breath was difficult, her back straight as an arrow, but her senses swimming, and she was a little afraid now that she understood what Lord Rushington spoke of.

"Lord Rushington." Miss Glover spoke again, her words firm and clear. "Might I ask if you are speaking of the young lady whom you threw such harsh words at, one night at Almack's? It was some time ago, yes, but from what I recall, you were in your cups and –"

"Yes, yes, that is it!" Lord Rushington hurried forward, catching Miss Glover's hand, and setting both of his around it, looking down into her eyes with such a fierceness that Miss Glover dropped Julia's hand. "You know of what I speak?"

"Y – yes, I do."

Miss Glover glanced at Julia, who immediately shook

her head no, only for Miss Glover to do precisely the opposite of what Julia had wanted. To her mind, Lord Rushington was in such a frantic state, he did not seem to be in the best mind to listen to her explanations – but yet, Miss Glover seemed determined.

"When you say that you have attempted to turn things to rights, do you mean –"

"I have already gone to Lord Harbison's townhouse in search of Miss Morningside," Lord Rushington said, interrupting Miss Glover's question. "She was absent, as was her mother. I left my card, but I have every intention of returning there, within the hour. I understand that they were only to be gone for a short time, and I *must* speak with them both. After what I have learned about my behavior and the consequences which she has faced thereafter, it is the only thing I can think of."

Miss Glover nodded, then looked pointedly at Julia.

"I am certain that both myself and Miss Smith understand you," she said quietly, as Lord Rushington dropped Miss Glover's hands, stepping back but lowering his head, his hands tight and curled at his sides.

"And you will then understand why I must take my leave." A hiss of breath followed Lord Rushington's words. "Pray forgive me but I -"

"What you *must* do, Lord Rushington, is to speak to Miss Smith."

Miss Glover's voice rent the air, louder than a thunderclap to Julia's ears. She watched as Lord Rushington stopped, his feet having been turned towards the carriage, only for him to swivel carefully back towards them. His eyes went first to Miss Glover and then, with infinite carefulness, returned to Julia.

It was a struggle to hold his gaze.

"You tell me that I must speak with Miss Smith?" Lord Rushington frowned, though he did come back towards them. "Why should that be?"

Miss Glover smiled gently, her eyes glistening as she looked from Lord Rushington to Julia and then back again.

"Because she has much to tell you." Her shoulders lifted, then fell. "Is that not so, *Miss Smith*?"

Julia tried to speak but the words seemed somehow caught in her throat and thus, she merely nodded but dropped her gaze. Lord Rushington's presence grew closer, she could practically feel the warmth from his body as he came near her. Another glance up told her that Miss Glover had melted away, leaving Julia and Lord Rushington as alone as they could be, given the circumstances.

Which meant that she had no other choice but to tell him the truth.

"I do not understand." Lord Rushington's voice had a slight catch to it. "Why should I speak to you? What is it that you know of this situation?"

All of a tremble, Julia looked up into Lord Rushington's face, taking in the serious set of his blue eyes, which had darkened considerably since the last time she had seen them.

"It is as Miss Glover says." Her voice was high-pitched, her words hurried. "I have much to say as regards the situation. That was why I wrote to you."

"Are you closely acquainted with Miss Morningside?" Lord Rushington asked her, coming a little closer until his breath fell upon her cheek. "Or are you related in some way? Is that what your letter meant? Perhaps she is a dear friend and has told you of this affair – and if that is the case, I must beg of you to permit me an introduction to her. I have only words of profound apology to offer her."

Julia tried to speak but, yet again, her words were thick in her throat, refusing to come forth. Her eyes went down to her feet, her heart trembling as she took a breath, one hand curling into a tight fist to help her garner a little more composure.

"You are distressed."

Lord Rushington sounded confused, and as she dared lift her gaze to him, she saw the way that his eyes danced around her face, seeking to find the answer to his confusion written there.

"I am." Julia closed her eyes tightly, shutting out the sight of him in the hope that it would finally allow her to tell him the truth. "Lord Rushington, you say that you seek to make amends?"

"Of course I do." Lord Rushington's voice had grown a little lower. "I was heartbroken over what I had discovered. Miss Davenport had betrayed me, and the pain within me was, I felt, almost unbearable. I had imbibed a good deal that evening and, on seeing a person who I believed to be Miss Davenport – though my vision was somewhat fuzzy – I spoke to her in the harshest manner. The gentleman she was with removed himself from her side almost at once, and I found my heart leaping about with gladness because of it."

Julia opened her eyes and looked at him but this time, *he* was the one not looking back at her. His head was turned to one side, his jaw tense and lips pinched as he paused in silence for a few moments. She understood now just how deeply he felt the guilt over his actions.

"I was then gone to my estate for my sister's marriage to her long awaited betrothed, and did not know whether I would return to London. When I did come back, Lord Burnley made it quite plain to me that the lady I had roared at with such cruel, harsh words was *not* Miss Davenport.

Even then, I spoke with him and convinced myself that there was nothing I needed to do. Society was not speaking of the matter any longer, and I presumed, foolishly so, that there would be a realization that it was Miss Davenport whom I had been betrothed to, *not* Miss Morningside." His head lowered and he put one hand over his eyes, his breath hissing out of clenched teeth. "I was selfish and inconsiderate, thinking only of my own pain. Too late, I have realized that this Miss Morningside will have suffered because of my actions. That is why I beg of you, Miss Smith, if you know of her, if you are acquainted with her, then pray, please tell me what I must do, to be of aid to her, to heal the damage which I have done."

His hand dropped, but instead of falling back to his side, it reached out for hers, his fingers warm on her cool skin. A flurry of heat wound its way up from where their hands met, and forced her gaze back to his. The fervency in his eyes demanded that she respond and, with a tremble shaking every part of her, Julia opened her mouth and told him what he needed to hear.

"Yes, Lord Rushington, I am acquainted with Miss Morningside." Her eyes closed again, a single tear falling to her cheek. "More than acquainted with her. I know her completely." Swallowing hard, she summoned all of her courage and looked him straight in the eye. "*I* am Miss Morningside."

CHAPTER SEVENTEEN

*B*enedict couldn't speak. A wave of shock had crashed into him and rendered him completely, unable to speak. Miss Smith – or as he now knew her to be, Miss Morningside, looked at him with wide eyes, the green orbs darkening a little – though whether from fright or fear, he could not be sure.

She is Miss Morningside?

If only he had realized it before! There it was before him now, the reason that she had kept herself away from society, the reason that he had struggled to find her at any society event. She had enjoyed the Vauxhall Gardens and the Masquerade, but both events had permitted her to hide away, first in the darkness of the Gardens and secondly, behind her mask.

And I did this to her.

"You are Miss Morningside?" His breath rasped as he spoke, watching her as she nodded but said nothing more thereafter. Rubbing at his eyes, he blinked back at her as if, in doing so, she might drift away from him, and he might discover the last few minutes had been nothing more than a dream. She remained firmly in front of him. "Might I ask if you knew that I was the one who had railed at you?"

Miss Morningside closed her eyes again, just as another tear fell to follow the first one, which had been swiped away.

"Yes, Lord Rushington. I knew."

"From the beginning of our acquaintance?"

"Yes." Her eyes did not open, nor look up at him. "From the beginning of our acquaintance, I was aware of precisely who you were and what you had done."

Benedict's confusion grew steadily.

"Then why did you acquaint yourself with me? I do not understand."

"Might I suggest that we walk?" Miss Glover's voice had Benedict starting in surprise, for he had forgotten that she was present. "There may come some discussion if anyone notices that we are standing about together but with only the two of you in obvious conversation."

Benedict nodded and moved away, but did not offer his arm to Miss Morningside as he would usually have done. It was as though his feet made no sound as he walked, and he felt light and weak, such was his shock in reaction to her response.

"You asked me why I acquainted myself with you." Miss Morningside's voice was quiet, winding up towards him as he glanced at her, only to pull his gaze away again. "If you wish to know the truth, then I shall tell you."

"I wish to hear it."

There was a harshness to his voice now which he did not attempt to pull back. Why had she spent so long in his company if she had known that he was the one who had injured her so? It did not make sense.

Miss Morningside took a deep breath, letting it sigh out of her before she continued.

"The evening when the incident occurred, I was at one of my very first few balls. I was to dance with Lord Charleston. I was happy and excited to be finally be given the opportunity to step out and find my place in society, just as my elder sister had done. However, in coming face to face with you, by your words, all of my hopes were instantly smothered. What both you and thereafter, your sister, said to me did not go unnoticed by the *ton*. Within only a few hours, I was pushed away by society, left to wallow in consequences which I did not deserve." All of this was said without any anger in her voice, only a heavy sadness that Benedict felt sweep over him, also. How much she must have suffered! How much she had been forced to endure – and all because of him. "My father had, by this time, returned to his estate, for he had matters which were very pressing indeed and he could not spare the time to be in London for a prolonged period. Therefore, it was left to my mother and myself to attempt to find a way through this difficulty."

"And did you succeed?" The shock which had carried him away was beginning to release him, softening and then fading away, bit by bit, until his heart began to feel all manner of things again. Seeing her look up at him quickly, he took his gaze from her again, a swell of embarrassment burning through him. "No, of course you did not."

"I *could* not." Miss Morningside let out another small sigh. "The *ton* turned against me and pushed me back into the shadows. I have become a wallflower, Lord Rushington, for that is all I am now considered worthy to be." Again, no malice flooded her words, her face did not color furiously, and her voice did not rise with anger. Instead, she pulled out her handkerchief and dabbed at her eyes, pain clearly clawing at her. "My father suggested that we return to the estate and try to regain some standing in society next Season, but I did not want to for, by then..." Her voice faltered and she kept her head low. "By then, I had been introduced to you and I had made a specific decision as regarded you."

"A decision?"

Benedict pressed his lips flat, forcing himself to stop speaking, refusing to ask anything of her, despite the dozens of questions which began to pour into him. Her voice was already thin, shaking with an obvious struggle, and he would not permit himself to interrupt her.

"When we first became acquainted, when I told you that we had already been introduced and that you had forgotten my name – that was nothing but a falsehood. I waited to see if there was a flash of recognition in your eyes when you saw me but was then keenly disappointed. You did not know who I was."

"I do not fully understand it myself," Benedict muttered, shaking his head. "There are some similarities between yourself and Miss Davenport, certainly, for you both have dark hair and green eyes, but beyond that, there is nothing that would make one think that you were the same."

Miss Morningside's lips curved into a small, sad smile.

"I presume, in your somewhat altered state, that it would have been difficult to distinguish."

"That is true." Wincing at how foolish he had been, he looked away from her again. "But what I said to you that night, none of that is true of you. I am truly sorry for what I did."

"I understand, and I am grateful to hear you say so."

Miss Morningside dabbed at her eyes again, her steps slow. "However, the reason I did not give you my real title was because, at that point, I had an intention all of my own." A heady color began to rise into her face, though she did not look at him again. "I wanted you to feel the same pain as that which I had endured, to suffer in much the same way as I had done. Those words sound utterly dreadful upon my lips, now that I speak them, but that is the truth."

Benedict stopped, turning so that he could face her. Waiting, he lingered close to her, not speaking a word until she had lifted her head and finally looked at him.

"I do not blame you for those desires, Miss Morningside."

Her eyes closed again, as though she could not bear to hold him in view for more than a few moments.

"I was angry and upset, Lord Rushington." Her voice was nothing more than a whisper now. "I could not understand why you had said nothing to me. I thought that you must have realized your mistake and then, to see that you did not recognize me was a fresh agony to my heart. Miss Glover did try to encourage me to push away from revenge, telling me that it would not be a wise path, but I ignored her."

"But you have done nothing to me." Benedict reached out and took her hand, pressing it firmly and praying that she would not pull away. "There has been no cruelty on your part, save for pretending that you had told me your title when, in reality, you had not."

Miss Morningside nodded, and when she spoke, her words were thick with tears.

"I could not bring myself to do as I had planned," she told him, her bonnet hiding much of her face as her head fell forward. "My intentions were strong but instead, I began to realize the difficulties of doing as I had planned. I would cause injury to myself, as well as to you, and I could not allow my heart such suffering."

A flare of light pushed upwards through Benedict's heart and his fingers twined through Miss Morningside's, effectively pulling her to him.

"What retaliation had you planned for me, Miss Morningside?" When she shook her head, he stepped a little closer, aware that they stood in the middle of the park in clear view of anyone who had decided to walk that afternoon, but heedless to what they might think of them. "Tell me, my dear lady. I will not be injured by it, I assure you. I already accept that I deserved a good many consequences over my foolishness!"

Miss Morningside brought her eyes to his once more. They were glistening with tears, her heart clearly pained over what she had to tell him. Taking a deep breath, she set her shoulders back, though her lips trembled still.

"I thought to be as flirtatious and as tantalizing as I could so that you might fall in love with me." Her eyes closed again. "And I fully intended to pull back from you abruptly, once a declaration had been offered me. I wanted your heart to smash, to break asunder so that you too would feel something akin to the suffering I have endured from being pushed back by society." Her eyes opened again. "In saying those things to you, I see now the depths of my pain, but also the horror of my intentions. I deeply regret even *thinking* of that, Lord Rushington. Of course, it was also why I did not tell you my name, for fear that you would have already heard it, and that you would realize that I was the lady whom you had mistaken for Miss Davenport. I did not want you to know of that, until I was ready, until the moment came when I might reveal all. You cannot know how ashamed I am of my actions."

Benedict smiled. Miss Morningside's eyes flared in surprise, as she took in his expression, and was confused by it.

"I should say, Miss Morningside, that you have succeeded in your intentions." One hand lifted her chin gently, not wanting her to hide her face from him any longer. "I was perturbed by my feelings at first, not because I thought there to be anything wrong with our connection, but simply because I had already believed myself to be in love before. However, the longer I spent with you, the more I understood the difference between you, Miss Morningside, and Miss Davenport. With Miss Davenport, I had allowed my heart to fill with her beauty, without even knowing her character. I had based my reactions on a few stolen moments and brief conversations, but that was all. When I proposed to her, it was without knowing the truth of her character. If I had given myself a little more time, had told myself to consider matters a little more, then I might have realized how foolish and hasty I was being, and then I would not have been so brokenhearted when I saw her as she truly was!" With a scowl, he shook his head and looked away. "But then, once I considered you, and realized how often I had been in your company, how long we had talked, how much I appreciated your conversation, and how happy I was when I had you on my arm... I saw then how different it all could be." His hand dropped back to his side. "When you kissed me, I had to admit it to myself. I had to admit what it was that my heart felt."

Miss Morningside shivered, her eyes still on his face.

"What was it that you felt, Lord Rushington?"

"Love." The word came easily enough, but sat between

them, a heavy boulder which could not be ignored. "I see now that I love you, Miss Morningside – and you do not know how frustrated I was because of it!" A quiet laugh escaped when she frowned. "After that kiss, I wanted to find you, I wanted to learn the truth and speak with you of what my heart was saying, but I could not."

"Because you did not know my name." Miss Morningside nodded, looked away and then, for what seemed to be the first time in an age, she let a smile touch one side of her mouth. "I understand." Blinking, she bit the edge of her lip. "I did want to speak with you about it all, Lord Rushington. That was why I wrote to you. It had all grown into such a confusion, I had no choice but to begin to sort out each strand – and that began with telling you the truth."

"Which you have done now, in its entirety."

She nodded, confirming this.

"Then we are at ease with each other," he said softly, his fingers still pressed through hers. "I must apologize to you now, profusely, for the shame I placed upon you – a shame which you had no reason to bear. I cannot imagine what this must have been like for you, these last few weeks."

Miss Morningside took a long breath, then managed to smile – this time, without tears shimmering in her eyes.

"It has been difficult, but not solely for the reason you might think. Yes, I was absent from society, and no longer received as many invitations as I had done before, but the more time I spent in your company, the longer I was with you, talking and laughing and conversing, the more I found my heart troubled over what I had intended to do." With another small sigh, her smile grew even more, and she moved a little closer, her eyes searching his face. "You have quite stolen away my heart, Lord Rushington. I could not bring myself to separate from you in the way that I had planned, for it would have shattered my heart and soul. I did not want to place such pain upon myself. I confess I feared that when I came to tell you the truth, you would turn away from me, regardless, and I would suffer that sorrow anyway, but I contented myself with the knowledge that I would have told you the truth, as well as acknowledging to myself that your reaction would be the consequences of my actions."

"The only consequences, my dear Miss Morningside, are that my heart is now entirely and completely your own." Taking her hand, he lifted it to his lips and pressed a soft kiss to it, hearing her snatch in her breath as he did so. "And I fully intend that each and every gentleman and lady within the *ton* will know of it... just as soon as possible."

CHAPTER EIGHTEEN

Julia pressed her hands to her stomach as she looked at her reflection in the mirror. Yet again, she was wearing her mother's diamond pendant, dressed in her finest gown, and prepared for entering society again, but the nervousness within her was like nothing she had ever experienced before.

"My dear." Lady Harbison entered and stopped almost the moment she set foot inside, her hands clasped at her heart. "How beautiful you look."

Julia managed a smile, her heart leaping furiously as she turned to face her mother.

"Thank you, Mama. Are you quite certain that father will be contented with it all?"

"Yes, I am." Lady Harbison looked back at Julia, grasping her shoulders lightly. "I wrote to him and, whilst there has not been time for him to respond, I can assure you that his response will be a positive one."

Julia swallowed tightly, her fears still lingering.

"But if he does not understand about what has happened as regards Lord Rushington, then –"

"He will." Her mother's hands dropped back to her sides, her smile still fixed and filled with confidence. "You explained all to me some three days ago now, as did Lord Rushington and, whilst I will confess to being overcome with surprise, my heart soon flooded with delight and happiness, for now I know that my daughter will not only be happily married but that her reputation will once more be as it ought. I was most glad to see that he is no longer the rather foolish young man he was last Season – he seems most intent on doing everything honorable."

"We are not betrothed yet, Mama."

A warmth came to Julia's cheeks, but her mother only laughed quietly.

"I am well aware of that, my dear, but I have seen the way that Lord Rushington looks at you. I think him more than a little overcome, and I am quite certain that what he spoke of, regarding his feelings for you, will only grow all the more, until he has every intention of proposing. I think that you will be betrothed within the month!" The heat in Julia's face ran down her chest and into her stomach, where it pooled and curled deliciously, sending a smile to her lips. "And your father will accept him," Lady Harbison continued before Julia could even think to ask such a question. "Have no concern in that regard. I confess I am looking forward to this evening, and to what Lord Rushington intends to do!"

Julia laughed, though the sound came out a little unevenly.

"I am very nervous indeed, Mama. We return to Almack's, where the very incident took place!"

"You need not be so." Coming closer to her again, Lady Harbison shifted the diamond necklace just a little. "After all that you have suffered, and all that you have endured, you have found happiness at the end of it all. Lord Rushington is an excellent gentleman, and I say with confidence that he will be able to take care of you for the rest of your life."

Julia nodded, turned, and looked at her reflection once more. This was to be her first step back into society as a lady loved by Lord Rushington. This was to be the evening when the *ton* would hear all, where they would accept her back into their fold without hesitation. Her name would, no doubt, be on the lips of everyone, come the morrow, but this time, for an entirely different reason. They would speak of her connection to Lord Rushington, of her new courtship, and of how she had been mistaken for another. And then, in time, there would come news of her betrothal and subsequently, her marriage. The confidence that her mother expressed was within Julia also, for the love she shared with Lord Rushington was not one that would simply fade away. It possessed her, which had taken such a hold of her, that it would never depart from her again – and she trusted his heart was the same.

"I am ready, Mama." With a breath, she turned back to face her mother, who was now battling tears of happiness. "Come now. Let us go."

∽

"Miss Morningside."

Julia smiled and clutched at her friend's hand, seeing Miss Glover smile.

"You no longer have to refer to me as 'Miss Smith', I suppose," she said, with a small smile. "I am very grateful to you for all that you have done in aid of me, and for your presence here this evening. I confess to being filled with nervousness!"

"You have nothing to be anxious about." Miss Glover let out a small, contented sigh. "All will be made right. I am sure that you will have a flurry of apologies made to you in the time thereafter! Your mother also will certainly have some prior acquaintances returning to her."

Julia wanted to say more, to state how unfortunate it was that the *ton* were so willing to believe what they were told, only to be distracted when a hand touched her shoulder. The flurry of excitement that ran down her arm and to her fingers gave her every indication of who was beside her.

"Rushington."

"My dear lady." Lord Rushington caught her fingers, then bowed low over her hand as Miss Glover stepped tactfully away. "Might I say just how beautiful you look this evening? I think that every eye will be upon you and that all of the gentlemen within my sphere will be jealous that *I* am the one who has you in my arms."

"You are very kind." A frisson of nervous excitement made its way through her, and she clutched his hand a little tighter. "I am sure that nearly every eye is upon me already, for they will all be wondering why you would be speaking with the lady who spurned you so terribly."

"And," Lord Rushington smiled, his eyes darkening as a whirlwind rushed around Julia's frame, "they will wonder why I am not only bowing over your hand for the second time but also why my lips are now pressed to your skin."

The warmth of his lips on hers jolted her and Julia's eyes fluttered closed for a moment, only for her to hear Lord Rushington chuckle.

"I think that we will have caught the attention of many,"

he murmured, stepping closer to her now, their hands the only thing separating them. "You must excuse me now, but I *shall* return to you... and very soon."

Julia could only hold his gaze, saying nothing as she watched him move away. Their eyes held for as long as they were able, broken apart by the swirl of gentlemen and ladies moving around the room.

"Do you have any knowledge of what he intends to do?"

Shaking her head, Julia let a long breath settle her somewhat, though her hand which had been held captive in Lord Rushington's for so long was now wrapped around her waist.

"No, but I trust him."

"Which is just as you should." Miss Glover smiled, just as Lady Harbison returned to join them.

"Has all gone well?" She put one hand to Julia's waist, her eyes searching her face. "I saw Lord Rushington approach you, and held myself back. I will say, there were a good many eyes upon him as he spoke with you, and I heard one or two exclamations when he bowed over your hand!"

She beamed with evident delight as Julia laughed gently.

"I believe that he thought it might garner some interest," she said, as her mother chuckled. "He has excused himself, though I do not know what he is to do. He said that he would return momentarily, and promised that, very soon, the *ton* would seek to pull me back into their embrace and that you, Mama, might receive a good many apologies from acquaintances who have pushed you back these last few weeks."

Lady Harbison rolled her eyes.

"I do not think that I want any such apologies." A purse of her lips indicated her displeasure. "I would not consider anyone who threw me away in such a careless manner, without even having the grace to speak with me about it first, to be a delightful acquaintance." Her eyes flashed. "There have been a great many truths revealed this Season, and I intend to be very cautious as to who I consider to be a close acquaintance, from this moment onward. "

"Which makes me all the more grateful for your stalwart friendship, Mary." Julia caught her mother nodding fervently as Miss Glover waved one hand, as though to say that she did not think her actions at all significant. "I may have returned to my father's estate had it not been for you."

"I am very glad that you did not."

With a smile, Miss Glover made to say more, only for a small, tinkling sound to catch her attention. Frowning, Julia turned her head, looking all around the room for the sound. The conversation and the laughter soon began to fade away as the tinkling sound continued, until almost everyone had fallen silent.

"Pray excuse the interruption." In an instant, all of Julia's body burned hot as Lord Rushington's voice filled the empty space. "I understand that all of you wish to dance, and converse and the like, but I must speak to all who are present here and express to you, quite clearly, that I have been a fool." At this, there came some murmurs and titters of laughter, but Julia only stared, willing the crowd to part so that she might lay eyes upon Lord Rushington. As if they had heard her thoughts, two gentlemen moved away and instantly, her eyes caught those of Lord Rushington. "Some time ago, I stood in this very ballroom and fixed my gaze upon a young lady. I believed that she had done me a great wrong."

Julia closed her eyes and let out a slow, careful breath,

sensing dozens of eyes turning to look at her, the hair on the back of her neck beginning to prickle.

"I was mistaken."

There came an audible gasp from those standing close to Julia, and she opened her eyes, just as her mother took her hand in her own and squeezed it tightly.

"Much to my current chagrin, I was deeply in my cups at the time, and I made my way across the room to the middle of the dance floor and berated this young lady. I told her that she was the worst sort of creature, that she had broken my heart and injured me most severely. I am certain that many here will know of what I speak! In addition, I informed everyone – in speaking to her as I did – that she had broken her betrothal to me by making her way into the arms of another."

Taking a deep breath, Lord Rushington put one hand out towards Julia and almost every head turned to look directly at her. Her face hot, Julia clamped her gaze upon Lord Rushington, refusing to permit herself to look anywhere else but into his eyes. He was her strength, her anchor. If she dared to let her gaze drop, then she might sink away forever.

"Ladies and gentlemen, I am here this evening to inform you all that the young lady I railed at, the young lady I threw such terrible words at, was none other than Miss Julia Morningside – and she did not deserve a single one of my sharp arrows. She was *not* the young lady I was betrothed to. She had never even been introduced to me!"

Lifting her chin, Julia finally allowed her gaze to rove around Almack's. It seemed as if hundreds of eyes were fixed on her now, and she looked into as many as she could. Some ladies had their hands at their mouths, their expression one of utter horror, whilst others immediately began to whisper to the person next to them. Lord Rushington went on, his voice steady.

"In my drunken state, I did not realize that I had made such a mistake. Having spoken those terrible words, I made my way home and, thereafter, returned to my estate so that my sister could be wed. When I later made my way back to London, I was informed that the lady I thought I had spoken to had been somewhere else entirely at that time, and to my shame, I realized my mistake, but chose to do nothing to correct it. In my mind, I believed that the gossip would have removed itself from the unfortunate young lady and that she would now be recovering from what would only have been a mere embarrassment." Knotting his brows together, Lord Rushington scowled. "I was wrong. You had all chosen to push her away, to cut her company, to force her to retreat. She became a wallflower, forgotten by some, but ignored by nearly everyone. To her, I owe a great apology and I should like to state, here and now, that Miss Julia Morningside has done nothing worthy of censure – that censure was due to an entirely different young lady. I was mistaken and, in turn, led all of you to believe that a great wrong had been done to me by Miss Morningside. I hope, now that I have explained, that you will return her to your company and no longer push her into the shadows."

With a nod to indicate that his small speech was complete, Lord Rushington turned, snapped his heels together, and bowed in Julia's direction. He lingered there for a few moments longer than was expected and Julia's eyes immediately began to burn with tears. The whispering and the murmuring began almost at once, but as Lord Rushington rose to his full height, that sound fell away. Julia could no longer hear it, letting herself be filled with only the sight of him as he came towards her.

"I must pray that you will accept my apology."

Julia laughed just as tears sparked in her eyes.

"Oh, my dear Lord Rushington. I do not think that there is anything in the world that would keep me from accepting it." Her hand went to her heart. "You cannot know how much I value what you have done."

"I do hope it means that you will be restored to your rightful situation," he told her, before taking a small side step and bowing low again, looking at Lady Harbison as he rose. "And to you, Lady Harbison, I must express my apology and my regret also. It was never my intention to injure Miss Morningside, and my remorse over my actions is very great indeed."

Lady Harbison smiled at him as Lord Rushington lifted his head.

"Lord Rushington, you have done a great wrong, certainly, but you have done all that you can, now, to make it right. I would not hold back my forgiveness from you. Indeed, I do not think that I could even try to do so, given how much my daughter has come to care for you!"

Julia blinked her lingering tears away, her face scarlet as she looked from her mother to Lord Rushington and back again. Her mother had spoken clearly and, no doubt, those who stood nearby, and who were able to hear her would now begin to whisper such news to others. Had there not been enough gossip for one evening?

"Do not be too concerned." Lord Rushington grinned at her, and Julia tried to smile back, catching the edge of her lip between her teeth. "I can see that you are concerned, but I assure you, you need not be. We are to be courting, are we not? It is just as well that the *ton* know of it, for then, very soon, they will find something else to discuss and we will find ourselves forgotten."

"Which is exactly what I desire," Julia murmured, trying not to allow her gaze to dart around Almack's. "I have been stung by gossip, so I am a little concerned, I admit. I do not wish to feel that attention again."

Lord Rushington chuckled, then as the music began, bowed to her again.

"The only way to battle gossip is to give it something else to feed on – even if we are to be the delicious morsel it chews upon for a while. Come now, Miss Morningside. Will you dance with me?"

Julia smiled up at him, took his hand and, in that one moment, it was as though there were no others present in the room but him. As he led her out to the center of the dance floor, she kept her gaze fixed, not wanting to break apart the moments of calm he offered her, simply by looking back into her face.

"It is at an end, Julia," he murmured, as the dance began. "The gossip, the whispers, the pain, the shunning. It is all at an end."

"Yes. It is. Already my heart feels lighter." As they were forced to step apart for a brief moment, her fingers burned to once more catch his within her own. "Thank you for what you did."

"What else could I do but rescue the lady I put into difficulty?" Lord Rushington's eyes grew serious, his smile faded. "I care so very much for you, Julia. You are my very heart."

"As you are mine."

As the dance continued, neither she nor Lord Rushington said anything more. Instead, they simply danced together, their gazes fixed, and their hearts filled with a happiness that they both shared, one which spread from his heart to her own – and one which Julia was certain could never be taken away. No matter what it was that they would face, she would have Lord Rushington beside her, holding her close, holding her tight, and loving her more and more with every moment that they shared together.

What more could she ask for?

EPILOGUE

"Lord Rushington." Benedict threw a glance at Miss Morningside as Lady Guthrie now turned her attention towards her. "And Miss Morningside. Goodness, what a difficult situation you found yourself in! It must have been very trying."

Miss Morningside drew herself up a little, and Benedict caught the way that her fingers pulled more tightly around his arm.

"Yes, it has been exceptionally difficult, Lady Guthrie, made all the more so by those who would not listen to my, or my mother's, explanations and instead, chose to listen to gossip, and gave us the cut direct thereafter."

A little surprised by the slight edge to Miss Morningside's words, Benedict looked directly at Lady Guthrie who, in turn, went a very delicate shade of pink. Her eyes snapped to Benedict and then returned to Miss Morningside.

"I can see how difficult that must have been," she answered, sniffing lightly. "I am glad to know the truth of it now, of course."

"I am certain that my mother would be glad to hear you say such a thing also."

Lady Guthrie's smile was a little tight.

"But of course. I shall make my way to her directly, I think."

As she walked away, Benedict turned and saw that Miss Morningside's face was a little red, though when she caught his eye, a small, wry smile spread across it.

"Forgive me for being so sharp."

"I quite understand. I assume that she was one of the ladies who did not speak to you after what took place?"

Miss Morningside nodded, her eyes drifting back towards Lady Guthrie who had made her way across the room to speak with Lady Harbison.

"She has long been an acquaintance of my mother. When she gave me the cut direct and thereafter, refused to even acknowledge my mother, I saw the pain which her actions brought."

"Which you did not permit her to forget."

"Do you think I ought not to have done so?" Miss Morningside moved towards him a little more, her fingers curling about his arm, her green eyes a little wider still – and Benedict smiled.

"No, I do not. I am glad that you had the strength to speak so openly and honestly with her. I think that your mother will be glad of it also."

Miss Morningside closed her eyes and let out a slow breath, smiling briefly before opening them again.

"I do hope so. Mother has been such a stalwart support and I did not like to see her so troubled." Her smile returned. "It seems that all will be well again, however." Tilting her head, she lifted one eyebrow gently. "Or, I should say, it seems as though it will be even better than before, in fact."

Benedict chuckled, finding the desire to wrap his arms around her growing so strong that it was difficult indeed not to do so, even though they stood in the middle of Almack's.

"I promise you, I shall do everything that I can to make it so, my dear lady." The strength of his smile faded to tenderness as his hand found her free one and clasped it gently. "I do not think that I shall ever find as much happiness as I do when I am with you, Julia. You have brought such joy into my life, and I shall do all that I can to return such joy to you."

Before she could answer, music began to swell. Stepping back, Benedict gestured to the dance floor – the very one where they had first faced each other, where he had ruined himself entirely in her eyes.

"The waltz, my Lady?"

Miss Morningside's eyes were filled with smiles and, as she inclined her head in acceptance, Benedict's heart filled itself with her once more. They stepped out together, ignoring everyone else who stood with them, and yet Benedict was all too aware of just how many people would be watching them. This evening had been one of revelation, and he was overwhelmed by how much happiness he had been left with.

The music began and Benedict swept Miss Morningside into his arms. It was not the first time that they had waltzed, but it felt as if he were standing up with her for the very first time. His first waltz had been with 'Miss Smith' but, on this occasion, he knew her exactly as she was. She was Miss Julia Morningside, the young lady who had stolen his heart away, and from whom he never wished to take it back again.

The warmth in her eyes drew him towards her, his breath coming all the quicker as the dance continued. The music flowed, ebbing, and rising again to a crescendo as he held her a little closer than was expected, seeing the soft glow of her eyes, and knowing what it spoke of.

It spoke of a tenderness, of a love which he trusted would never be extinguished. How much he cared for her! Even the thought of separating from her at the end of the evening was a dark one, and he hated the distance between them, every moment that they were apart.

I want to marry her.

The thought was not unexpected, and did not come with a great deal of surprise. The music continued and Miss Morningside looked up at him still, her smile growing gently.

"There is something in your face which I cannot quite make out," she murmured, as the music began to slow, indicating the end of the dance. "What is it that you are thinking of?"

Benedict did not answer, but when the music finished, once they separated and then came together again, he led her away from the dance floor, but did not stop until he came to a door. Not knowing what was behind it, but glad that Miss Morningside was willing to go with him, he pushed it open and stepped inside.

"Miss Morningside." They stood in a hallway, only a door away from the rest of the guests, but with enough privacy for them to speak alone. "Julia."

"Yes, Rushington, I am here."

His hand went to her face, his fingers running across her cheek, then dropping to the column of her throat. She did not say a word, but he heard her hitch of breath and smiled gently down at her. He would take no liberties here, would not push himself forward and demand anything from her. All he wanted to do was to speak from his heart.

"I love you, Julia."

"As you have my love also." One hand lifted to settle on his shoulder, the other still free by her side, and Benedict reached for it, wanting to have her fingers twine through his again. "There need not be any more apologies or the like, Rushington. I do not want to think of the past any longer."

"Nor do I," he promised her. "Instead, I want only to think of our future. You will recall how I told you that I proposed to Miss Davenport after only a short acquaintance?"

Miss Morningside nodded.

"I do recall you speaking of it, yes."

"Then I want you to understand that, when I ask *you* to marry me, it is not with any of the same feelings which I had for Miss Davenport." Miss Morningside's eyes rounded, a gasp issuing from her mouth, but Benedict only squeezed her fingers a little more tightly. "I did not love Miss Davenport," he told her, as her fingers tightened on his shoulder. "I see that now, because what I feel for you has such strength, such power, and such a hold over me, that I cannot break free of it. It has become a part of me, melding into my heart and filling it with nothing but you. The thought of stepping away from you this evening, wondering when I will next be in your company, brings me such dismay, it is almost a pain in my heart. Therefore, I want us to keep such separations to a minimum."

Miss Morningside's smile slowly began to lift, and Benedict's heart lurched with the anticipation of overwhelming happiness.

"I would like to marry you, Julia. I want to take you as my bride, to make you my wife. I do not want to be held back from you any longer. I want you as mistress of our estate, to have a home and happiness with you, to build our lives together, and to build that upon the love we both share. What say you, Julia?" Moving a fraction closer, he put one hand on her waist. "Will you marry me?"

Miss Morningside closed her eyes, but her smile grew so quickly. It was as if the sunlight had broken through the night sky, through the roof itself, and shone down upon them. Benedict's heart leaped, and he pulled her a little closer, only for Miss Morningside's eyes to open and her hand to lift from his shoulder to press against his cheek.

"There is nothing which could separate me from you, Rushington. Nothing which would encourage me to refuse." Her fingers trailed gently down his face until her hand wound around his neck instead. "I love you with all of myself. There is nothing that would make me happier than to be your wife."

Benedict dropped his head and kissed her, allowing himself a moment of pure sweetness where there was nothing separating them. Passion roared to life, but he held it captive, refusing to permit it free. Such things were joys still to come, and for now, he wanted only to be present in this moment, contented in the knowledge that, very soon, the lady he loved would stand beside him as his bride.

"When?" Their kiss broke and Miss Morningside's eyes fluttered open, her cheeks a little flushed. "When will we marry?"

"Just as soon as it can be arranged," he promised her, his voice soft with tenderness. "I shall set to work on it come the morrow. Will that satisfy you, my love?"

Miss Morningside leaned into him, her head going to his chest, resting against the steady beat of his heart.

"Yes, my dear Rushington," came her murmured reply.

"But I shall count every day until I am able to stand up in church and make a promise to be your own for as long as I live." Her head tilted and she smiled at him. "For that is what I shall do. I shall love you and hold you to my heart for every day that I draw breath. I love you, Rushington."

"As I love you, Julia."

I am so glad Julia got her happy ever after. I felt so bad for her!

Did you miss the first book in the series? Read on for a preview. The Wallflower's Secret

MY DEAR READER

Thank you for reading and supporting my books! I hope this story brought you some escape from the real world into the always captivating Regency world. A good story, especially one with a happy ending, just brightens your day and makes you feel good! If you enjoyed the book, would you leave a review on Amazon? Reviews are always appreciated.

Please go to my website for a list of all of my books! There are a lot of them!

Rose Pearson Books in Order

Check out my Facebook Group for contests and free books!

Rose's Ravenous Readers

Happy Reading!
All my love,
Rose

A SNEAK PEEK OF THE WALLFLOWER'S UNSEEN CHARM

PROLOGUE

"You must promise me that you will *try*."

Miss Joy Bosworth rolled her eyes at her mother.

"Try to be more like my elder sisters, yes? That *is* what you mean, is it not?"

"And what is wrong with being like them?" Lady Halifax's stern tone told Joy in no uncertain terms that to criticize Bettina, Sarah, and Mary – all three of whom had married within the last few years – was a very poor decision indeed. Wincing, Joy fell silent and dropped her gaze to her lap as her beleaguered lady's maid continued to fix her hair. This was the third time that her lady's maid had set her hair, for the first two attempts had been deemed entirely unsuitable by Joy's mother – though quite what was wrong with it, Joy had been completely unable to see.

"You are much too forward, too quick to give your opinion," her mother continued, gazing at Joy's reflection in the looking glass, her eyes narrowing a little. "All of your elder sisters are quiet, though Bettina perhaps a little too much so, but their husbands greatly appreciate that about them!

They speak when they are asked to speak, give their opinion when it is desired and otherwise say very little when it comes to matters which do not concern them. *You,* on the other hand, speak when you are *not* asked to do so, give your opinion most readily, and say a great deal on *any* subject even when it does not concern you!"

Hearing the strong emphasis, Joy chose not to drop her head further, as her mother might have expected, but instead to lift her chin and look back steadily. She was not about to be cowed when it came to such a trait. In some ways, she was rather proud of her determination to speak as she thought, for she was the only one of her sisters who did so. Mayhap it was simply because she was the youngest, but Joy did not truly know why - she had always been determined to speak up for herself and, simply because she was in London, was not, she thought, cause to alter herself now!

"You must find a suitable husband!" Exclaiming aloud, Lady Halifax threw up her hands, perhaps seeing the glint of steel in Joy's eyes. "Continuing to behave as you are will not attract anyone to you, I can assure you of that!"

"The *right* gentleman would still be attracted," Joy shot back, adding her own emphasis. "There must be some amongst society who do not feel the same way as you, Mother. I do not seek to disagree with you, only to suggest that there might be a little more consideration in some, or even a different viewpoint altogether!"

"I know what I am talking about!" Lady Halifax smote Joy gently on the shoulder though her expression was one of frustration. "I have already had three daughters wed and it would do you well to listen to me and my advice."

Joy did not know what to say. Yes, she had listened to her mother on many an occasion, but that did not mean that she had to take everything her mother said to heart... and on this occasion, she was certain that Lady Halifax was quite wrong.

"If I am not true to who I am, Mama, then will that not make for a very difficult marriage?"

"A difficult marriage?" This was said with such a degree of astonishment that Joy could not help but smile. "There is no such thing as a difficult marriage, not unless one of the two parties *within* the marriage itself attempts to make it so. Do you not understand, Joy? I am telling you to alter yourself so that you do *not* cause any difficulties, both for yourself now, and for your husband in the future."

The smile on Joy's face slipped and then blew away, her forehead furrowing as she looked at her mother again. Lady Halifax was everything a lady of quality ought to be, and she had trained each of her daughters to be as she was... except that Joy had never been the success her other daughters had been. Even now, the thought of stepping into marriage with a gentleman she barely knew, simply because he was deemed suitable, was rather horrifying to Joy, and was made all the worse by the idea that she would somehow have to pretend to be someone she was not!

"As I have said, Joy, you will try."

This time, Joy realized, it was not a question her mother had been asking her but a statement. A statement which said that she was expected to do nothing other than what her mother said – and to do so without question also.

I shall not lie.

"I think my hair is quite presentable now, Mama." Steadfastly refusing to either agree with or refuse what her mother had said, Joy sat up straight in her chair, her head lifting, her shoulders dropping low as she turned her head from side to side. "Very elegant, I must say."

"The ribbon is not the right color."

Joy resisted the urge to roll her eyes for what would be the second time.

"Mama, it is a light shade of green and it is threaded through the many braids Clara has tied my hair into. It is quite perfect and cannot be faulted. Besides, it does match the gown perfectly. You made certain of that yourself."

So saying, she threw a quick smile to her lady's maid and saw a twitch of Clara's lips before the maid bowed her head, stepping back so that Lady Halifax would not see the smile on her face.

"It is not quite as I would want it, but it will have to do." Lady Halifax sniffed and waved one hand in Clara's direction. "My daughter requires her gown now. And be quick about it, we are a little short on time."

"If you had not insisted that Clara do my hair on two further occasions, then we would not be in danger of being tardy," Joy remarked, rising from her chair, and walking across the room, quite missing the flash in her mother's eyes. "It was quite suitable the first time."

"*I* shall be the judge of that," came the sharp retort, as Lady Halifax stalked to the door. "Now do hurry up. The carriage is waiting, and I do not want us to bring the attention of the entire *ton* down upon us by walking in much later than any other!"

Joy sighed and nodded, turning back to where Clara was ready with her gown. Coming to London and seeking out a suitable match was not something she could get the least bit excited about, and this ball, rather than being a momentous one, filled with hope and expectation, felt like a heaviness on her shoulders. The sooner it was over, Joy considered, the happier she would be.

CHAPTER ONE

"And Lord Granger is seated there."

"Mm-hm."

Nudging Joy lightly, her mother scowled.

"You are not paying the least bit of attention! Instead, you are much too inclined towards staring! Though quite what you are staring at, I cannot imagine!"

Joy tilted her head but did not take her eyes away from what she had been looking at.

"I was wondering whether that lady there – the one with the rather ornate hairstyle – found it difficult to wear such a thing without difficulty or pain." The lady in question had what appeared to be a bird's nest of some description, adorned with feathers and lace, planted on one side of her head, with her hair going through it as though it were a part of the creation. There was also a bird sitting on the edge of the nest, though to Joy's eyes, it looked rather monstrous and not at all as it ought. "Surely it must be stuck to her head in some way." She could not keep a giggle back when the lady curtsied and then rose, only for her magnificent headpiece to wobble terribly. "Oh dear, perhaps it is not as well secured as it ought to be!"

"Will you stop speaking so loudly?"

The hiss from Lady Halifax had Joy's attention snapping back to her mother, a slight flush touching the edge of her cheeks as she realized that one or two of the other ladies near them were glancing in her direction. She had spoken a little too loudly for both her own good and her mother's liking.

"My apologies, Mama."

"I should think so!" Lady Halifax grabbed Joy's arm in a somewhat tight grip and then began to walk in the opposite direction of that taken by the lady with the magnificent hair. "Pray do not embarrass both me and yourself, with your hasty tongue!"

"I do not mean to," Joy muttered, allowing her mother to take her in whatever direction she wished. "I simply speak as I think."

"A trait I ought to have worked out of you by now, but instead, it seems determined to cling to you!" With a sigh, Lady Halifax shook her head. "Now look, do you see there?"

Coming to a hasty stop, Joy looked across the room, following the direction of her mother's gaze. "What is it that you wish me to look at, Mama?"

"Those young ladies there," came the reply. "Do you see them? They stand clustered together, hidden in the shadows of the ballroom. Even their own mothers or sponsors have given up on them!"

A frown tugged at Joy's forehead.

"I do not know what you are speaking of Mama."

"The wallflowers!" Lady Halifax turned sharply to Joy, her eyes flashing. "Do you not see them? They stand there, doing nothing other than adorning the wall. They are passed over constantly, ignored by the gentlemen of the *ton,* who care very little for their company."

"Then that is the fault of the gentlemen of the *ton,*" Joy answered, a little upset by her mother's remarks. "I do not think it is right to blame the young ladies for such a thing."

Lady Halifax groaned aloud, closing her eyes.

"Why do you willfully misunderstand? They are not wallflowers by choice, but because they are deemed as unsuitable for marriage, for one reason or another."

"Which, again, might not be their own doing."

"Perhaps, but all the same," Lady Halifax continued, sounding more exasperated than ever, "I have shown you these young ladies as a warning."

Joy's eyebrows shot towards her hairline.

"A warning?"

"Yes, that you will yourself become one such young lady if you do not begin to behave yourself and act as you ought." Moving so that she faced Joy directly, Lady Halifax narrowed her eyes a little. "You will find yourself standing there with them, doing nothing other than watching the gentlemen of London take various *other* young ladies out to dance, rather than showing any genuine interest in you. Would that not be painful? Would that not trouble you?"

The answer her mother wished her to give was evident to Joy, but she could not bring herself to say it. It was not that she wanted to cause her mother any pain, but that she could not permit herself to be false, not even if it would bring her a little comfort.

"It might," she admitted, eventually, as Lady Halifax let out another stifled groan, clearly exasperated. "But as I have said before, Mama, I do not wish to be courted by a gentleman who is unaware of my true nature. I do not see why I should hide myself away, simply so that I can please a suitor. If such a thing were to happen, if I were to be willing to act in that way, it would not make for a happy arrangement. Sooner or later, my real self would return to the fore, and then what would my husband do? It is not as though he could step back from our marriage. Therefore, I would be condemning both him and myself, to a life of misery. I do not think that would be at all agreeable."

"That is where you are wrong." Lady Halifax lifted her chin, though she looked straight ahead. "To be wed is the most satisfactory situation one can find oneself in, regardless of the circumstances. It is not as though you will spend a great deal of time with your husband so, therefore, you will never need to reveal your 'true nature', as you put it."

The more her mother talked, the more Joy found herself growing almost despondent, such was the picture Lady Halifax was painting of what would be waiting for her. She understood that yes, she was here to find a suitable match, but to then remove to her husband's estate, where she would spend most of her days alone and only be in her husband's company whenever he desired it, did not seem to Joy to be a very pleasant circumstance. That would be very dull indeed, would it not? Her existence would become small, insignificant, and utterly banal, and that was certainly *not* the future Joy wanted for herself.

"Now, do lift your head up, stand tall, and smile," came the command. "We must go and speak to Lord Falconer and Lord Dartford at once."

Joy hid her sigh by lowering her head, her eyes squeezing closed for a few moments. There was no time to protest, however, no time to explain to her mother that what had just been discussed had settled Joy's mind against such things as this, for Lady Halifax once more marched Joy across the room and, before she knew it, introduced Joy to the two gentlemen whom she had pointed out, as well as to one Lady Dartford, who was Lord Dartford's mother.

"Good evening." Joy rose from her curtsey and tried to smile, though her smile was a little lackluster. "How very glad I am to make your acquaintance."

"Said quite perfectly." Lord Dartford chuckled, his dark eyes sweeping across her features, then dropping down to her frame as Joy blushed furiously. "So, you are next in line to try your hand at the marriage mart?"

"Next in line?"

"Yes." Lord Dartford waved a hand as though to dismiss her words and her irritation, which Joy had attempted to make more than evident by the sweep of her eyebrow. "You have three elder sisters do you not?"

"Yes, I do." Joy kept her eyebrows lifted. "All of whom are all now wed and settled."

"And now you must do the same." Lord Dartford chuckled, but Joy did not smile. The sound was not a pleasant one. "Unfortunately, none of your sisters were able to catch my eye and, alas, I do not think that you will be able to do so either."

"Dartford!"

His mother's gasp of horror was clear, but Joy merely smiled, her stomach twisting at the sheer arrogance which the gentleman had displayed.

"That is a little forward of you, Lord Dartford," she remarked, speaking quite clearly, and ignoring the way that her mother set one hand to the small of her back in clear warning. "What is to say that I would have any interest in *your* company?"

This response wiped the smile from Lord Dartford's face. His dark eyes narrowed, and his jaw set but, much to

Joy's delight, his friend began to guffaw, slapping Lord Dartford on the shoulder.

"You have certainly been set in your place!" Lord Falconer laughed as Joy looked back into Lord Dartford's angry expression without flinching. "And the lady is quite right, that was one of the most superior things I have heard you say this evening!"

"Only this evening?" Enjoying herself far too much, Joy tilted her head and let a smile dance across her features. "Again, Lord Dartford, I ask you what difference it would make to me to have a gentleman such as yourself interested in furthering their acquaintance with me? It is not as though I must simply accept every gentleman who comes to seek me out, is it? And I can assure you, I certainly would not accept you!"

Lord Falconer laughed again but Lord Dartford's eyes narrowed all the more, his jaw tight and his frame stiff with clear anger and frustration.

"I do not think a young lady such as yourself should display such audacity, Miss Bosworth."

"And if I want your opinion, Lord Dartford, then I will ask you for it," Joy shot back, just as quickly. "Thus far, I do not recall doing so."

"We must excuse ourselves."

The hand that had been on Joy's back now turned into a pressing force that propelled her away from Lord Dartford, Lord Falconer, and Lady Dartford – the latter of whom was standing, staring at Joy with wide eyes, her face a little pale.

"Do excuse us."

Lady Halifax inclined her head and then took Joy's hand, grasping it tightly rather than with any gentleness whatsoever, dragging her away from the gentlemen she had only just introduced Joy to.

"Mama, you are hurting me!" Pulling her hand away, Joy scowled when her mother rounded on her. "Please, you must stop—"

"Do you know what you have done?"

The hissed words from her mother had Joy stopping short, a little surprised at her mother's vehemence.

"I have done nothing other than speak my mind and set Lord Dartford – someone who purports to be a gentleman – back into his place. I do not know what makes him think that I would have *any* interest in—"

"News of this will spread through London!" Lady Halifax blinked furiously, and it was only then that Joy saw the tears in her mother's eyes. "This is your very first ball on the eve of your come out, and you decide to speak with such force and impudence to the Earl of Dartford?"

A writhing began to roll itself around Joy's stomach.

"I do not know what you mean. I did nothing wrong."

"It is not about wrong or right," came the reply, as Lady Halifax whispered with force towards Joy. "It is about wisdom. You did not speak with any wisdom this evening, and now news of what you did will spread throughout society. Lady Dartford will see to that."

Joy lifted her shoulders and then let them fall.

"I could not permit Lord Dartford to speak to me in such a way. I am worthy of respect, am I not?"

"You could have ignored him!" Lady Halifax threw up her hands, no longer managing to maintain her composure, garnering the attention of one or two others nearby. "You did not have to say a single thing! A simple look – or a slight curl of the lip – would have sufficed. Instead, you did precisely what I told you not to do and now news of your audacity will spread through London. Lady Dartford is one of the most prolific gossips in all of London and given that you insulted her son, I fear for what she will say."

Joy kept her chin lifted.

"Mama, Lady Dartford was shocked at her own son's remarks to me."

"But that does not mean that she will speak of *him* in the same way that she will speak of you," Lady Halifax told her, a single tear falling as red spots appeared on her cheeks. "Do you not understand, Joy?"

"Lord Falconer laughed at what I said."

Lady Halifax closed her eyes.

"That means nothing, other than the fact that he found your remarks and your behavior to be mirthful. It will not save your reputation."

"I did nothing to ruin my reputation."

"Oh, but you did." A flash came into her mother's eyes. "You may not see it as yet, but I can assure you, you have done yourself a great deal of damage. I warned you, I *asked* you to be cautious and instead, you did the opposite. Now, within the first ball of the Season, your sharp tongue and your determination to speak as you please has brought you into greater difficulty than you can imagine." Her eyes closed, a heavy sigh breaking from her. "Mayhap you will become a wallflower after all."

Hmm, my mother always said my mouth would get me into trouble…and now Miss Bosworth could be in trouble! Check out the rest of the story from the link on my website! Rose Pearson Books in Order

JOIN MY MAILING LIST

Sign up for my newsletter to stay up to date on new releases, contests, giveaways, freebies, and deals!

Free book with signup!

Monthly Facebook Giveaways! Books and Amazon gift cards!
Join me on Facebook: https://www.facebook.com/rosepearsonauthor

Website: www.RosePearsonAuthor.com

Follow me on Goodreads: Author Page

You can also follow me on Bookbub!
Click on the picture below – see the Follow button?

202 | JOIN MY MAILING LIST

Printed in Dunstable, United Kingdom